ALMOST FIFTEEN

ALMOST FIFTEEN

Marilyn Sachs

Oxford University Press
Oxford Toronto Melbourne

Oxford University Press, Walton Street, Oxford OX2 6DP

Oxford New York Toronto
Delhi Bombay Calcutta Madras Karachi
Petaling Jaya Singapore Hong Kong Tokyo
Nairobi Dar es Salaam Cape Town
Melbourne Auckland

and associated companies in
Berlin Ibadan

Oxford is a trade mark of Oxford University Press

Copyright 1987 by Marilyn Sachs

First published in the United States by E. P. Dutton,
a division of NAL Penguin Inc.
Published simultaneously in Canada by
Fitzhenry & Whiteside Ltd, Toronto
First published in the UK by Oxford University Press, 1988

Reprinted 1989

British Library Cataloguing in Publication Data

Sachs, Marilyn
    Almost fifteen.
    I. Title
    813'.54 [F]   PS3569.A2/
    ISBN 0-19-271597-6

Printed and bound in Great Britain by
Biddles Ltd, Guildford and King's Lynn

for three of my favorite allergics—
    Ruth Hadlock
    Tammy Halperin
        and
    Laurence Yep

Chapter 1 ❧

"*Drop dead!*" *I tell him.* "*We're all finished.*"

"*No, Imogen, please,*" *he says, grabbing my arm.* "*Just let me explain.*"

"*Get your hands off me,*" *I cry, struggling to free myself.* "*Let me go.*"

"*Imo! Imo!*" *There are tears in his eyes, and I can hear his voice breaking.*

"*Rodney Freeman,*" *I say, brushing his hands off my arm and pushing him away,* "*you're a jerk and I'm sick of you.*"

"No!" a child yelled, "I don't want to be here. I want to go home. I want to go home."

I was sitting in my allergist's office waiting for my shot, and had been passing the time daydreaming about my boyfriend, Rodney, and about how I wanted to break up with him.

"Now, Bobby, Mommy's going to get you a nice surprise after we leave," said a nervous-looking woman who was seated across from me in the waiting room, and was trying to hold on to a struggling little boy of about five.

"Yes, Rodney, I'm sick of you because you're selfish and inconsiderate and because you're . . ."

"No, no, no!" Bobby screeched, "I want to go home."

I disentangled myself from the daydream, and smiled at Bobby. Poor kid! I could still remember the way I felt eight years ago when I was six, and my mother brought me to Dr. Rovensky's office for the first time.

"He's never been here before," Bobby's mother explained in a loud whisper to her neighbor, an interesting-looking boy about my own age whom I had never noticed before in the office. The boy mumbled something and edged away from her.

Big tears rolled down Bobby's face, and suddenly he began hiccuping. His mother took off his jacket and murmured some comforting words about treats and chewing gum. Bobby stopped struggling, slumped against her, and looked hopelessly around the room. Some of the regulars like Mrs. Foster and Mr. Helling smiled and nodded at him. When his eyes finally rested on me, I was ready. I smiled but I also wiggled my ears.

It worked. It always worked. Bobby gave one huge hiccup and straightened up, his eyes focused on my

2

ears. I wiggled them again, and Bobby put up a hand and touched one of his own ears.

"Well, will you look at that," said Bobby's mother. "Will you just look at how the nice girl can wiggle her ears."

Bobby looked and so did the boy sitting next to him. For a moment our eyes met, he nearly smiled, and then he ducked down behind a magazine. I felt a warm tingle as I wiggled my ears again. In a few minutes, Bobby had moved away from his mother and was standing in front of me. I went through my routines—from ear wiggling to tongue curling to finger lacing.

"My goodness," Bobby's mother said, "you certainly have a way with children."

> Here's the church
> And here's the steeple.
> Open the door
> And out come the people.

Bobby's fingers entwined themselves with mine, and we went through the routine together.

"Do you ever baby-sit?" his mother asked.

"Yes, I do," I told her. "I baby-sit a lot."

"Well, where do you live?"

"In the Richmond district," I told her, "on Twenty-fourth Avenue."

"That's wonderful," she said. "We're over on Lake and Ninth. I could come and get you and bring you home. Or you could sleep over." She had a hungry look as she watched Bobby climb up onto my lap. From long experience with prospective clients, I could tell that the hungrier the look on the parent's face, the harder the kid. "What's your name anyway? I'm Jeanette Jackson."

"How do you do, Mrs. Jackson. My name is Imogen Rogers."

"Hello, Imogen."

"But everybody calls me Imo," I said, managing to get in a quick glance at the interesting-looking boy whose eyes were fixed on his magazine. He had dark curly hair, wore glasses, and might have been fifteen or even sixteen.

Adrian, the nurse, came out of the office and called, "Bobby Jackson!"

Mrs. Jackson stood up. "Come on, dear. Dr. Rovensky wants to see you."

"No," Bobby yelled. "I want to stay here." He began hiccuping again.

"You go with your mother, Bobby," I said, "and I'll tell you a secret."

"What secret?" Bobby asked.

I pulled him over. Poor little guy! I could hear him wheezing as I bent over and whispered in his ear.

"Oh?" Bobby said and smiled. He took his mother's hand, and she turned to me and said urgently, "Don't go away, Imo. I want to talk to you."

"What did you tell him, dear?" Mrs. Foster asked after they had been absorbed into the office.

"I told him that Dr. Rovensky has one blue eye and one brown eye."

"I never noticed," said Mr. Helling.

A sound—maybe a muffled laugh or a snort—came from the direction of the boy. Mr. Helling leaned over

4

toward me and whispered, "There's a lot of new people here today."

"I know," I whispered back.

Mr. Helling, Mrs. Foster and I were the old-timers in Dr. Rovensky's office. I had been coming for allergy shots every third Wednesday since I began eight years ago. Mr. Helling claimed that he was Dr. Rovensky's first patient, and Mrs. Foster said she was married to a man whose sister married and divorced Dr. Rovensky's first cousin. The three of us knew a lot about each other.

"I remember you when you were that child's age," Mrs. Foster said, smiling at me, "and here you are fourteen years old. How time does fly!"

"Almost fifteen," I corrected her. "I'll be fifteen in May."

"You were so cute," Mrs. Helling continued, "a little chubby thing with a big mop of hair. And your nose always ran and you kept wiping it on the back of your hand. . . ."

Adrian emerged from the office just in time. I was sure Mrs. Foster was going to reminisce about the time I wet my pants. "Mark Feller," she called. The boy stood up. He was tall, I noticed approvingly, and quite thin, not like little, pudgy Rodney Freeman.

I looked after him as he slouched into the office. His posture could be better, I thought, but tall people often slouch. Me, for instance. At nearly five feet ten, I always slouch. Especially when I hang around with Rodney Freeman, who's barely five feet eight.

I suppose I had been slouching when I caught up with Rodney in the hall earlier today at school.

5

"Hey, Rodney, wait a minute."

"Oh . . . Imo . . . oh!" he said. "Uh . . . I . . . uh."

"What happened to you last night?" I asked him, quite friendly. Not in a nasty way at all. "Your mother said you were helping your father carry a chest up the stairs and that you'd call me back."

"Well . . . it was a big chest."

"She said you'd call me right back. I waited around all evening."

"I . . . uh . . . I had to help him carry up a mirror too."

"Anyway, Rodney," I said, "I wanted to tell you we can go with Melissa and Jeff on Saturday."

"Saturday?" Rodney's face twisted itself up in bewilderment.

"Saturday," I repeated. "You remember, Rodney. Carrie's party on Saturday. All the kids from the chorus are going after our concert at Masonic Hall."

"Oh, Saturday," Rodney gasped. "That's right. Saturday!"

"Saturday," I said encouragingly. "So now that Jeff has his license, his mother says he can have the car. He'll pick us all up after the concert. You can come over to my house for dinner before if you like."

I stood there beaming at him, and slouching over, but he just seemed to crumble, and the expression on his face changed from bewilderment to horror.

"Saturday," he moaned.

I guess that was the time I decided to break up with him. He hadn't been the same ever since Mrs. Powers changed my place in the chorus and moved me into the sopranos. Last term, I had sung with the altos, and Rodney, who was a tenor, stood right next to me. That's how our romance began, as we sang "When the Foe-man Bares His Steel" from *The Pirates of Penzance*. But everything had changed over the past three weeks. Now Brenda Jacobson stood next to him. She's one of those little, bone-headed girls with a voice that's hardly ever on key. My friend Melissa said she saw Rodney and Brenda eating sushi together in Kyoto's on Clement Street. He never ate sushi with me. Not that I could eat sushi with him anyway, since I'm allergic to fish.

Mrs. Jackson stuck her head out of the office and called, "Imo, give me your name and address. We're going to be here for a while, and I don't want to lose you."

"She's wonderful with children," Mrs. Foster said. "She gets lots of baby-sitting jobs from parents who see her in action here at the office."

"Oh dear," Mrs. Jackson said. "I hope you're free Thursday nights and Saturdays. I could use you steady on those nights, and sometimes on Sundays too."

Mark Feller came out of the office, rolling down his sleeve. I could feel the warm tingle behind my ears again, even though he didn't look in my direction as he moved on out through the door.

"Uh . . . well Thursdays are usually fine, but Saturdays might be a problem. I handed Mrs. Jackson a paper with my name, address, and phone number on it.

"Can you sit for me this Saturday?" she asked.

"Well, no, I can't."

"I'll call you, Imo. We'll work something out." Mrs. Jackson turned and hurried back into the office.

"Mr. Helling," Adrian called out.

7

The office was beginning to empty. Mrs. Foster started giving me the details of her latest skin rash, and I settled back in my chair and pretended to listen. But I was thinking of Rodney. Of how I would call him that night and end it.

Chapter 2 ❧

My grandmother's door was open. As usual. I stuck my head inside and yelled, "Lin Lin! Your door is open."

Nobody answered. She had obviously gone out and forgotten to close her door. I keep reminding her and reminding her, but all she ever does is launch off into a long story about how nobody ever locked doors in San Francisco when she was a child, and how even though things have changed for the worse since then, in all the sixty-one years of her life behind unlocked doors, nobody has ever robbed her.

I closed her door as I always did, unlocked our door, and climbed up the stairs. We live in a four-family house that belongs to my family—to my grandmother actually. She lives downstairs below us, and Mr. and Mrs. Sloane live in the downstairs apartment on the other side. Mrs. Sloane is a wonderful cook, and the good smells from her kitchen permeate the entire building.

Above the Sloanes lives our newest tenant, Adam Derman, who just moved in two weeks ago. He is an older guy, about my parents' age, and my grandmother told us he was divorced.

I could hear the phone ringing as I came up the stairs.

"Maryanne, is that you?" my father yelled out.

"No, it's me, Dad."

"Well, will you please answer the phone? I'm right in the middle of something."

"Okay. Hello," I said into the phone.

"Hello. Is that you, Imo?"

"Yes it is. Is that you, Rodney?"

"Yes it is."

A silence followed as I began to assemble all my lines for the big scene.

"Uh . . . Imo . . . I . . . uh . . ."

"Yes . . . well . . . Rodney . . . I . . . uh . . ."

"Look, Imo . . . I . . . uh . . ."

"No, Rodney . . . let me . . . uh . . ."

"Imo, I think we should break up," he said, very, very quickly.

"Well, damnit Rodney, so do I. And I thought so before you did."

"No, you didn't," Rodney said, "because I've been thinking we should break up ever since last Wednesday night, after rehearsals."

"Well, I wanted to break up with you since Monday," I told him. My nose began running as it often does when I get excited, and I was glad he wasn't there to see it.

10

"So why did you tell me Jeff was going to pick us up this Saturday night if you wanted to break up with me?" His voice had a nasty sound to it. What a mean little nerd he was!

"Because . . . because . . . because," I yelled, wiping my nose, "I wanted to tell you then it was all over, and I didn't want to embarrass you in front of other people."

"No," he said, "you're lying. And it was my idea first."

"It was mine," I shouted.

"I said it first."

"Because you knew I was going to say it."

I hung up and quickly dialed my friend Melissa's number. I knew I had to spread the word quickly before Rodney did. I looked at my watch. Two minutes before five.

"Hello."

"Hello, Melissa?"

"Yes. Imo?"

"Yes. Listen, Melissa, I just broke up with Rodney."

"You did?" Melissa said. "Have you been running? You sound breathless."

"Yes. No. I haven't been running, but I did just break up with Rodney about ten minutes ago, at about a quarter to five."

"That's funny, because he was telling Katie and Tony on the bus this afternoon that he was going to break up with you. I was sitting a couple of seats in front of them, and I could hear everything he was saying."

"Oh no!" I groaned.

"And then he said that he and Brenda Jacobson were going to Carrie's party together on Saturday night. He

11

said that he felt kind of bad about you because he knew you were crazy about him."

"Well, why didn't you turn around and say it wasn't so? Why didn't you say I was going to break up with him?"

"Imo, I didn't know you were going to break up with him. I thought you thought he was great."

"No, I didn't think he was great. I never thought he was great. And I'm sure I told you I wanted to break up with him. Some friend you are!"

"Imo . . ."

"I've got to go. Good-bye."

I knew I was being unreasonable with Melissa, and that later I would have to call her and apologize. But for now I needed to wallow in self-pity. Rodney Freeman had gotten the jump on me, and tomorrow all the kids at school would believe that he was the one who had broken up with me first. How was I going to survive tomorrow?

"Imogen," my father called.

"Yes?"

"Could you come in here a minute? I want to show you something."

Slowly I shifted into today and lumbered into my father's workroom. He was studying something on his big table, and he turned to smile at me as I came into the room. His face was rosy with excitement. "Just look at these proofs, Imo. Just look!"

I looked.

My father is a photographer, and his pictures hang all over our apartment. Most of them are scenic—waves breaking on beaches, sunsets over bays, pine trees on mountaintops. . . . All of them are out of doors, even the ones with people. There is one picture my father loves of my mother in deep shadow under a magnificent eucalyptus tree. Another one—which won third prize in a photography contest five years ago—shows two little girls in a field of daisies, putting flowers in each other's hair. I am one of the two girls, and Melissa is the other. It's my favorite picture and hangs in my bedroom.

"Well?" my father asked. "What do you think?"

I studied the proofs. They all seemed to be of large cliffs in bright sunshine.

"I think . . . I think . . . I think that tomorrow will be the worst day of my life."

I burst into tears.

My father said sadly, "You don't like them?"

"No, Dad," I wept. "It's not the proofs. They're beautiful. It's Rodney. Rodney Freeman. He just broke up with me. Before I could break up with him."

My father looked puzzled. "Rodney?" he said. "Rodney? Is that the one who tripped on his shoelace and broke his collarbone?"

"No, no," I sobbed. "You're thinking of Tim Krumgold. He broke up with me a year ago. Before I could break up with him. They always break up with me first." I stamped my foot. "It's not fair. It's not fair."

"Poor little Imo," murmured my father, gathering me up in his arms, and folding me into his lap. Even though he is only about my height and much slighter, I am always able to curl up comfortably in his lap.

"Everything will be all right, pumpkin," said my father gently, smoothing my hair. "You'll see. Everything always works out for the best sooner or later."

"You always say that," I wept, "but it's not true. At least it's not true for me."

"Sure it is," said my father, rocking me. "Should we go out and get some ice cream?"

"Of course not," I snapped. "What good would that do?"

"You always feel happy when you eat ice cream," my father said weakly.

"I'm not a baby anymore," I said angrily, straightening up and looking into his face. His blue eyes were troubled, and I felt ashamed. "Oh, don't mind me, Dad. I'll be all right."

"Sure you will," said my father, brightening.

"And I really like your pictures, Dad."

"Do you really, Imo? I think they're pretty good myself. One or two especially. The light was really incredible. I went back to Land's End today, and took some more. Maybe I'll submit the best ones to the museum for this year's annual show."

"But Dad, weren't you supposed to take pictures of the kids at the Peter Rabbit Nursery School?"

"Maybe next week I will. But first I need to get those pictures set for the show."

"But I thought the director of the nursery school asked you to come in today."

"I'll call her tomorrow and make a date for next week. I'm sure it will be all right. I'm not worried."

My father never worries—about money or anything else. He's been a free-lance photographer ever since he

14

graduated from college, which is why my name is Imogen. After the famous photographer, Imogen Cunningham. When people ask me what my father does for a living, I always say he's a free-lance photographer. And when I was younger, I felt proud to have a father who had such an interesting profession. It wasn't until I was ten or eleven that I began to realize that my father did not make a living with his photography. His pictures of the out-of-doors are beautiful, and sometimes they're even exhibited at various art galleries, but hardly anybody ever buys them. Occasionally, as in the case of the Peter Rabbit Nursery School, he might be offered a job because somebody involved is a friend of the family.

The truth of the matter is that nobody in my family makes a living—not my mother, not my father, and certainly not my grandmother. My grandfather, who died when I was ten, had been a gardener in his youth but gave it up a few years after he married my grandmother. He did handle the family finances, however, which got all scrambled up after he died. About a year ago, I began helping my grandmother sort things out, and now she wants me to take over. She has no head for figures, and neither do my parents. I do. I like adding up columns of figures and keeping records. I like feeling in control. That's why I plan on becoming an accountant.

I don't ever tell people that nobody in my family works for a living. It's embarrassing. How can I explain to other kids whose parents do work for a living that nobody in my family does? Melissa is the only one who knows, and she's sworn to secrecy. We live on royalties. From one book, a cookbook that my grandmother's aunt wrote many years ago. She never married, so when she died, my grandmother inherited all the rights to the book. It's called *The Friendship Cookbook,* and there's hardly anybody who hasn't heard of it. It's sold millions of copies, and we live off the royalties, which arrive twice a year. Some years are better than others, but there's always been enough for us to manage on. Until last year. The royalties last year were nearly as bad as this year. And I have a feeling that next year will be even worse. I worry about next year a lot. But I'm the only one in my family who does.

"I can't wait for your mother to see the proofs," said my father.

I stood up. "She's going to be a little late today because she promised to pick up some cheese ravioli at the factory after school. I may as well go and start the salad."

"Do you need me?" offered my father.

"No, not tonight. Tonight's Mom's night to cook. Tomorrow's yours."

"Oh no, not again!" moaned my father.

And that's another thing. Here we all are living off the royalties of a famous cookbook, but nobody in my family likes to cook. We all take turns and make easy things like ravioli, spaghetti, frozen chicken pies and tuna in cream-of-mushroom soup. My grandmother prefers hot dogs and hamburgers, and says she never could stand eating at her aunt's house when she was a child. That's the aunt who wrote the cookbook. I worry about that, too. It doesn't seem right that we should be living off the royalties of a famous cookbook when none of us likes to cook.

The door opened downstairs. "Hello-o-o!" shouted my mother.

"She's home," said my father. "Just wait until she sees my proofs."

My mother came running up the stairs, her books clutched against her chest, her dark eyes bright. "You'll never guess what just happened to me," she said and began laughing.

"Maryanne, I have something to show you," said my father.

"I was just putting my key into the lock," said my mother, "when Adam Derman, the new tenant, came up the stairs. Of course, I'd met him when he moved in, but I guess he forgot. Because he looked at me and then he asked me if I lived upstairs. I said yes. Then he told me that his little boy was coming to stay over the weekend, and he . . . he . . ." My mother was laughing so hard she couldn't finish.

My father started laughing right along with her even though he didn't know what was funny.

". . . he asked me," said my mother, taking a deep breath, "if I would baby-sit for him on Saturday night."

"That's crazy," I said. "Why did he do that?"

"Because he must have heard that there was a teenaged girl who lived upstairs, and he thought I was you. Now isn't that hysterical?"

I looked at my mother standing there in her pea coat, red plaid skirt, knee socks and flat shoes. I looked at her short, flippy dark hair; her smooth, pink cheeks; and her schoolbooks clutched against her chest. My heart was breaking, and my mother was standing there, grinning from ear to ear, because some stupid jerk couldn't tell the difference between a middle-aged woman and a teenaged girl.

"You're thirty-seven years old," I snapped at her, "but I guess you didn't tell him that."

"I did tell him that," said my mother, displaying a set of perfect white teeth. "I told him I was thirty-six (I'm not going to be thirty-seven, Imo, until next week), and a mother, and I said . . . I said . . ." My mother began giggling again.

"Well," I asked her crankily, "what did you say?"

"I said"—my mother wiped her eyes—"that I would ask you if you could baby-sit for him, and then he apologized. But I said he didn't need to feel bad because I didn't mind being taken for a teenager, and that I was sure you would be able to baby-sit."

"I have a concert Saturday night," I told her. "Didn't you remember that? And where's the cheese ravioli? I hope you didn't forget to pick up the cheese ravioli."

My mother waved a hand impatiently. "Oh, who cares about the cheese ravioli? I can run out and pick up some at the market. I had quite a day. Wait until you hear what else happened to me today."

"I can tell it was something good," said my father, looking at her shining face. "Well, what was it? Don't keep Imo and me in suspense."

"I'm not in suspense," I grumbled.

"Well, do you remember that test I had to take last Friday on Edmund Spenser's *Faerie Queen*?" Do you remember how I thought Professor Sheridan was planning to give that test on Monday, but when I went into class on Friday she began handing out papers, and I tried to explain to her that I hadn't studied because I thought the test was going to be given on Monday, and asked her if I could take a makeup?"

"And she said no," said my father sympathetically, "and you had to take the test, and you worried about it all weekend."

"Yes, yes." My mother's dark eyes sparkled. "Well, this morning before class, I met her in the hall, and she said to me, 'Ms. Rogers . . .' She's very formal, calls everybody Ms. or Mr."

"I'm hungry," I said.

"I'll go in a minute," said my mother. "Wait until you hear what she said. She said, 'Ms. Rogers, from now on, I would advise you never to study for future exams.' And when she handed the papers back, I got an A, and she wrote—wait until you see what she wrote."

My mother opened one of her notebooks and pulled out a paper. For as long as I can remember, my mother has been going to school. Currently, she's getting an M.A. in English literature, but she has another M.A. in ancient history, and a couple of B.A.'s as well.

My father took the paper and shook his head proudly as he read what Professor Sheridan had written.

"What's the use?" I said angrily. "I may as well go myself and get the ravioli. As usual, nothing ever gets done in this place unless I do it."

I went banging down the stairs and slammed the door going out. On the way to the store, I began feeling guilty. Why should I take out my anger on my wonderful mother who never raised her voice to me, just because Rodney Freeman was such a nerd. It wasn't her fault that he'd broken up with me. It wasn't her fault that everybody broke up with me sooner or later.

19

I was hurrying along too fast and could feel the wheeze expanding in my lungs. So I stopped, pulled my bronchial dilator out of my pocket and took a few puffs. Calm down, I told myself. Pull yourself together. It's not the end of the world. Think about some of the good things in your life.

Like what? Well, Mrs. Powers had put me in the soprano section in chorus and said I might sing a solo in the June concert. "Your voice has really developed," she said, "and you don't seem to have any trouble hitting the high notes." It made me feel so proud when she said it, and even if I did lose Rodney Freeman because she moved me out of the alto section, I had gained a soprano voice.

"Whose voice is it that soars above all the others like a nightingale among crows?"

"Oh, that's Imogen Rogers. Her voice has developed incredible richness in the past year."

"I want to meet her. I am a talent scout for the Metropolitan Opera Company, and . . ."

I bought a couple of packages of frozen ravioli and hurried home. Outside the Sloanes' door, I could smell something wonderful like mushroom-stuffed cornish hens. My grandmother's door was open, as usual, and I slammed it shut before going upstairs.

Chapter 3 ⟨❧

Melissa Gin has been my best friend since fifth grade. Sometimes, when we walk down the street together, people turn and look at us and smile. I am tall and large-boned, and she is small and dainty. We are an odd-looking combination, and we're also a study in contrasts. Melissa is self-assured, outspoken, very pretty and well dressed, while I . . .

"You," Melissa said firmly, the next day at school, "look like you're going to a funeral. Didn't I tell you to dress up today? Didn't I tell you to wear your bright red sweater and striped corduroy skirt? Didn't I?"

"Well, yes you did," I had to admit. Last night, when I called her back to apologize, she had already planned today's strategy.

"So? Why are you wearing that drippy navy blue sweater and that faded pair of black jeans?"

"Well, my mother has an early class, and she got the red sweater first—it's really hers anyway, Melissa, you know that—and the skirt has a big spot on it. My father was supposed to have done the laundry yesterday, but he's been very busy with his photography."

Melissa shook her head. "You look like death warmed over," she said. "It's a good thing we don't have chorus until last period. You can't let *him* see you looking like you're looking."

"Maybe I should go home," I suggested. "I really do have a stomachache."

"No," Melissa said. "You're not going home. You're going to wear my green snakeskin belt and . . ." She looked around the room. "There's Lori Corning. She's wearing a great Esprit vest, and she's just about your size. Stay right here! Don't move! I'll go talk to her."

By the last period, Melissa had me wearing Lori Corning's vest, Alison Yakawa's bright purple scarf, and her own green snakeskin belt. She had also plastered makeup all over my face and was coaching me furiously as we walked into chorus. "Now you just stand up straight, and keep your chin out. No slouching. No slumping. And when you see him, I want you to say, "Hi, Rodney," in a loud, very cheerful voice. Do you understand?"

"But Melissa . . ."

"No buts. Do you understand?"

"Well no, I don't. Why should I have to talk to him if I hate him so much?"

"I don't know, Imo," Melissa said. "You're supposed to be so smart. But for somebody who's supposed to be smart, you're really pretty stupid."

22

Rodney wasn't in chorus. Rodney was absent.

"Better yet," Melissa gloated. "Now you just go over and say hi to Brenda."

"No, I won't."

"Oh yes you will. And you say something loud about how you hope Rodney isn't too upset because you broke up with him. Go ahead! Now! Before Mrs. Powers stops talking to Glenda Rhys."

"Uh . . . hi . . . uh . . . Brenda," I mumbled.

"Oh . . . yes . . . Imo."

"Well," I said, "I hope . . . I hope . . . RodneyIhope heisn'ttooupsetbecauseIbrokeupwithhimlastnight."

"Who?" Brenda said.

"Never mind," Melissa said when I found my way back to the soprano section. "You did real well, and lots of kids heard what you said. And make sure to tell as many people as you can that you broke up with him before you go home today. So will I. He's not here to say anything different. By tomorrow, it will be too late."

That afternoon, I went home with Melissa to her small, pretty, neat house. Melissa is the youngest of four children and, as she admits herself, she is spoiled rotten. Her two older sisters and one older brother all still live at home. No wonder. Melissa's parents own a stationery store, but one or the other of them is usually at home directing the traffic. Everything runs smoothly in Melissa's house—meals are invariably served on time, laundries are always done, beds made, floors washed, cookies baked. . . .

"But they don't let me breathe," Melissa says whenever I complain about the difference between her house and mine.

"What do you mean they don't let you breathe? You have plenty of time to breathe. Your sister Angie bakes and cooks. Your sister Flora generally vacuums. Your brother, Hank, does all the grocery shopping. And your parents do everything else. All you have to do is be fussed over."

"I can't stay out as late as you," Melissa says. "And they always want to know where I am or who I'm with. Your folks don't hassle you that way. They treat you like an adult. They always treated you like an adult."

We were sitting in Melissa's breakfast room, a bright, sunny room with pots of blooming African violets at the window. Melissa was knitting herself a soft pink sweater out of some fuzzy wool, and I watched her fingers shoving the needles back and forth through the yarn.

"That's true," I said.

"And they never yelled at you or punished you. I mean, here I'm almost fifteen years old, and I was grounded last weekend because I didn't get home at exactly midnight on the dot. My father has some kind of Cinderella complex. If I'm not home at midnight, he thinks everything will fall apart. I keep telling him all the kids I know can stay out later, but it doesn't do any good. He's a real chauv when it comes to girls. Your father's not like that."

"No," I admitted. "He's not."

"See!" Melissa resumed her knitting. "And your grandmother's a doll. Both of my grandmothers complain all the time, but yours always seems to be having more fun than anybody else."

"I know," I said grimly.

"Do you remember the party she gave for you when

24

you were ten? Down in her house? Do you remember how we all made so much noise playing Blind Man's Bluff that the neighbor from next door came in because he thought something was wrong? And your grand-mother was laughing and yelling louder than anybody else? And do you remember the time she took us on BART to the Oakland Zoo and she got lost? And do you remember . . ."

"I remember. I remember," I told Melissa.

"I love your family," Melissa said seriously. "No-body's got a family like yours."

"I guess not," I said, "and I love them too, but . . ."

"But what?"

"Well—shouldn't they make a fuss like your father does if I come in late? They always say I know how to make the right decisions, and they never worry about me. But—shouldn't they? Aren't parents supposed to worry? And you know they're not like other parents. My father doesn't make any money at his photography, and my mother's always in school. How many mothers do you know who never leave school? It's weird. And my grandmother—she's like a kid. She never remem-bers to close her door, and she eats mostly hot dogs and hamburgers. She's sixty-one years old. She's not sup-posed to be like that. None of them worry about money. Except me. Last year the royalties on *The Friendship Cookbook* were terrible. This year, they're even worse. I'm worried about next year. I just don't know what will happen to all of us if the royalties get any smaller."

"You know something, Imo"—Melissa bit off a piece of the pink wool—"you worry too much. It's not natural for a girl your age to worry so much. You're supposed to be having fun. I don't understand it. Everybody else in your family has fun. Nobody else is worrying."

Which was true. I wish it wasn't.

"It makes you too serious. It gives you kind of a droopy look around the eyes."

"That's from my allergies."

"And sometimes you sound like you're an old woman instead of a young, pretty girl who's got a lot going for her."

I sniffed. "Do you really think I'm pretty, Melissa?"

"Of course you are. Especially when you stand up straight and wipe that tragic look off your face."

"But boys don't like me," I said. "Why don't they like me?"

"Now don't start that again." Melissa tugged at a piece of the yarn that had stuck. "I keep telling you that Leo Hassan likes you very much."

"He doesn't count," I said. "I'm talking about other boys."

"Well other boys like you too, and you've already had three boyfriends, which isn't a bad record. Some girls haven't had any. I've only had one."

"Yes, but he's lasted. He's been your boyfriend for nearly six months."

"Probably because he has to work after school so I only see him on weekends. Maybe if you see each other too much, it's no good."

"Do you think that's it?" I said, beginning to feel a little better.

"Sure." Melissa knotted two pieces of the yarn together. "You get tired of each other from too much togetherness."

26

"But they all get tired of me before I get tired of them," I said, feeling worse again. "And you can't really say I've had three boyfriends. Ben Ferguson was my boyfriend for only two weeks while we worked on that project about the Panama Canal for history. He was only interested in getting an A."

"But he *was* your boyfriend during that time," Melissa insisted.

"And Tim Krumgold lasted only six weeks, and Rodney Freeman two and a half months if you don't take off the two weeks he was away during the Christmas holidays," I said miserably.

Melissa held up her piece of pink sweater to my face. "This would be a wonderful color for you," she said.

That's the way she is, always changing the subject when it gets out of hand.

My grandmother's door was open when I got home. I stuck my head inside her apartment and yelled, "Lin Lin, your door's open." I knew she was home because her car was sitting in the driveway. No answer. I walked into her hallway, and then I heard the shower, which meant that she was probably going out to dinner. I could hear her singing Madonna's "Material Girl." A funny smell came from the kitchen, and I followed it over to a lopsided cake cooling on a rack. It's the only cake my grandmother ever bakes, and it's supposed to be the most famous recipe of all in *The Friendship Cookbook*. It's called a Friendship Cake, and Lin Lin says even her mother, my great grandmother, who also hated cooking, used to make it. I haven't checked the recipe in *The Friendship Cookbook*, but I think that somewhere along the line she's omitted a couple of ingredients or steps. Carefully, I backed away from it. Some poor host or hostess was going to be forced into eating it that very night.

Naturally, I closed her door before going upstairs. My father was in the kitchen, stirring a pot of spaghetti sauce.

"Mm, something smells good, Dad," I said. "Should I make the salad?"

"No, no," he said. "I've already made it. I figured we needed something special tonight."

There were opened cans all over the counters—kidney beans, artichoke hearts, anchovies, peas. . . . The kitchen sink was piled high with bowls, spoons, and pots. Somehow, whenever my father cooked, every dish and utensil within his reach came into play. The kitchen was a mess, but his sauce didn't smell too bad, and his face was rosy and cheerful.

"How's my little Imo?" my father asked. "Are you feeling better?"

I sighed. "I'm just fine, Dad. Just fine. I got through the day okay, thanks to Melissa."

"Melissa's a good friend," said my father, pouring spices into his sauce. "I've always liked Melissa."

"I know, Dad. She likes you too."

My father raised a spoonful of the sauce and tasted it. "Oh, this isn't too bad, Imo. Do you want a taste?"

"Sure, Dad." He blew on some of the sauce in his wooden spoon and held it out. "Be careful, Imo. Don't burn yourself."

The sauce was—interesting. It seemed to me I tasted cinnamon and maybe even some peppermint. But there was no point in asking. My father never remembered what he had put into his sauces. I gathered up the cans and carried them over to the refrigerator. Inside were four or five other opened cans from the last time my father had made the salad. I cleared them out, put in the new ones, and carefully closed the door.

"Is Mom back yet?" I asked. "Isn't today her early day?"

"I think so," said my father, whirling the pepper mill around over his sauce, "but she called about an hour ago to say a young woman in her class sprained her ankle, and she was going to take her home." My father turned around and shook his head. "You know your mother. She's always there when somebody needs help."

His voice was proud and loving. All the little tensions inside me melted away at the sound of my father's voice.

"Dad, did you . . . did you always love Mom?"

"Yes," he said solemnly. "I always loved her."

"Even when you were nine years old?"

"Even then," said my father. "When I first saw her in Mrs. Edwards's class in the fourth grade, with her ponytail tied with a pink ribbon and her pink socks, I loved her right away. I wanted to be her partner even though boys were supposed to be partners with boys, and girls were supposed to be partners with girls."

"I didn't know that," I told him, trying to think of my parents as fourth graders, and seeing them as they looked today, only a couple of feet shorter.

"In the fifth grade she didn't like boys, and she never even spoke to me. In the sixth grade she got chicken pox, and I took out a whole bunch of books on Argentina from the library for her and brought them over to her house. I thought she was doing Argentina for her report on South America, but she told me no, she wasn't. She said she was doing Brazil. So I had to take them all back again."

"Yes, yes," I said. "And then she changed her mind and decided to do Chile."

"Was it Chile?" said my father. "Or Paraguay?"

"It was Chile," I told him. "Go on, Dad. Tell what happened in eighth grade."

My father sat down beside me at the kitchen table, and the two of us immersed ourselves in memories of my parents' courtship. In eighth grade, my mother had defended my father when two bullies picked on him. In tenth grade, she had gone to a dance with a boy named Jim Cooper, and my father stopped speaking to her for three weeks. But the following year, she told him she guessed she would have to end up marrying him sooner or later.

"She told you?"

"Yes, she did." My father nodded his head. "You know that. She said she guessed she would end up marrying me because I had blond curly hair and she wanted . . . she wanted . . ."

"She wanted to have kids with blond curls and blue eyes," I said grimly.

My father reached over and stroked my dark hair. "That was before you were born," he said. "And I always wanted a little girl with dark hair and dark eyes."

"I'm not so little," I said, but I was feeling soft and

happy inside and, for the moment, not at all upset about the mess in the sink and the garbage bag I just noticed with something greasy oozing out from the bottom.

"But go on, Dad. Tell how you both used to meet each other between classes at San Francisco State, and how you used to sit on the steps between the second and third floor where you could hear the toilets flushing from the ladies' room. Tell how you got married when you both were twenty, and Mom wore a white nosegay with ribbons flowing down her back, and you wore an embroidered Russian shirt. And tell how I was born three years later and how you . . ."

"Wait, wait!" cried my father. "You left out the picnic on Mount Tamalpais."

My father and I were still sitting there by the kitchen table, both talking at the same time, when my mother arrived home.

"Mm! Something smells wonderful," she yelled even before she came flying into the kitchen. "How's everything?" she asked, sticking a spoon into the sauce and licking at it with her little pink tongue.

"Oh, just great," I said contentedly.

"Not so good," said my father.

"What's wrong?" my mother asked.

"Lin Lin," said my father gravely. "She got a ticket for speeding."

"Another one," I said sharply. "What happened this time?"

"Well, she said she really wasn't speeding but that something stuck in her accelerator."

"Nothing stuck in her accelerator," I said. "She said that the time before last, too."

"That's just terrible," said my mother. "Poor Lin Lin, this is the second time this year, isn't it?"

"The third," I said. "She went to traffic school once, and she'd better go again or the insurance company will refuse to cover her. Maybe they'll raise her rates anyway. Maybe she'll lose her license."

"She's very depressed," my father said.

"Poor Lin Lin," sighed my mother. "What can we do to cheer her up?"

"I invited her for dinner," said my father.

"Oh, that's nice." My mother smiled.

But I didn't smile. "She's bringing dessert, isn't she?" I demanded of my father.

"I told her not to bother," my father said. "But she insisted."

"You could have said no. You could have told her you had ice cream or a Sara Lee cake. You could have made up something.

"Oh dear," said my mother, "she must be bringing a Friendship Cake."

Chapter 4 &✦

Adam Derman rang the bell later that evening just after my grandmother had gone downstairs to watch *Dallas*. She had refused to take the remains of the Friendship Cake, and it was still lying there on the dining room table when my mother brought Adam into the room.

"Imo," my mother said, "Adam wants to know if you can baby-sit for him this weekend."

"I've already told you," I said to my mother, speaking very slowly and distinctly, "that I have a concert Saturday night."

"Yes," Adam said. "Your mother told me that, but I was wondering if you'd be able to sit on Sunday night. I'm willing to change my plans if you can. I want somebody I can trust."

I never turn down a baby-sitting job if I can help it.

Especially now that I'm so worried about next year's royalties. "Sure," I told him. "I can do it."

"Why don't you sit down and have a cup of coffee with us," my father said.

"I'd love to." Adam sat down right next to the Friendship Cake. "That cake looks interesting," he said to my mother. "Did you bake it?"

"Oh, no!" my mother said, escaping into the kitchen. "I'll get you some coffee."

"*My* mother made it," my father explained. "It's a very unusual cake, and it has a rather . . . unusual flavor. You're supposed to let the batter sit for a month or so outside of the refrigerator, and every day you stir it and add things to it."

"She always keeps a few bowls of that stuff around her house," I said. "We can't make her stop."

"Oh yes," Adam said, "like an old-fashioned fruit cake. My mother used to make one like that around Christmas. It was called a Friendship Cake. I loved that cake."

"Well," said my father, "this one's called a Friendship Cake too, but I have a feeling it doesn't taste the same as your mother's cake."

"She had a cookbook she got the recipe out of." Adam smiled. "She said it was her bible, and she was the greatest cook. She used to make mock turtle soup and chicken fricassee and old-fashioned lemon pudding."

"It's from the same book," my father said, "and if you think you'd like to try a piece . . ."

"Why sure," Adam said, holding his head on one side and inspecting the cake. "It doesn't look like my

34

mother's cake, but if it's a Friendship Cake, I'd love to try it."

"You don't have to," I told him.

He began laughing. "I was the same way when I was a kid," he said to my father. "I wanted to eat it all myself."

I stood up and followed my mother into the kitchen where she was pouring coffee into a mug. "He wants to try the Friendship Cake," I told her.

"Somebody should explain," she said.

"I tried, but he thought I didn't want to share it with him because it's so marvelous. Some people you just can't tell anything." I picked a clean plate and fork. "I'm going to cut him a real big piece."

"Now, Imo, don't be nasty," said my mother.

We all sat down and watched as Adam lifted a piece of the cake to his lips. He was telling us about how he used to live in Chico where he owned a service station, and how his former wife and little boy, Benjamin, still lived up there. Nobody said anything while he put the cake into his mouth and began eating it.

"Mm," he said, rolling it around in his mouth and slowly chewing it.

My mother spoke up first. "It's a very unusual cake."

"Yes," said my father. "My mother is a very unusual woman."

"Mm!" Adam said. It was taking him a long time to swallow.

"You can spit it out in the bathroom," I told him. "I always do when she's not looking."

Adam swallowed, but his face had turned an interesting shade of green. Carefully, he laid his fork down on the plate, and for a few moments was unable to say anything.

"I wonder if it's going to rain," said my mother.

The hardest part of breaking up with someone comes after it happens. Even though Rodney and I had only been going around together for two and a half months (if you include the two weeks he was away at Christmas), my life had settled into a going-together pattern. Most evenings we would talk to each other on the phone for a couple of hours, until his mother began yelling. Most afternoons he would wait for me or I would wait for him, and we'd take the bus together, except on the Wednesdays when I went to my allergist and Fridays, when he had oboe lessons. During chorus we would whisper little messages to each other, and once in a while, hold hands. Sometimes we'd go to parties with other kids in the chorus or just loll around my house. We'd talk about school and the classes we took together and the kids we both knew.

"That's not enough in a relationship," Melissa was saying. We both were at Carrie Schneider's party Saturday night after the concert. Carrie's sixteenth birthday fell on that very night, and her parents had invited the whole chorus to their house for a birthday celebration. There was plenty of food—cheese and cold cuts and long loaves of sourdough French bread. A big white-and-pink cake stood in the center of the table, wishing Carrie a happy birthday in pink icing. Mrs. Powers was drinking a glass of wine with Carrie's parents, and telling them how well the concert had gone. Everybody looked happy. Nearly everybody.

36

Some of the kids were dancing— Rodney and Brenda Jacobson, for instance, kept moving in front of me every opportunity they had.

"They're doing it on purpose," I said to Melissa.

"Ignore them," she said. "And besides, she isn't graceful at all. She's a real klutz. But anyway, he wasn't for you. He just never had the mental equipment for a girl like you. I never could understand what you saw in him. Now Leo is entirely different. . . ."

"You never said anything about Rodney to me before," I told her. "Only last week, you said you thought he was interesting."

"Sure I said that," Melissa answered. "Because how can you tell your best friend you think her boyfriend is a jerk? But whenever anybody uses the word interesting, you can be sure it's not a compliment."

Melissa's boyfriend, Jeff, said he wanted to leave soon.

"I think I'll leave when you do," I said

Rodney and Brenda hove into view again, laughing into each other's faces.

"I think you should stay," Melissa said.

"Why do I have to stay?"

"Because everybody will think you're having a lousy time if you leave when we do."

Along came Rodney and Brenda again, shaking every shakable part possible.

"Well, I am having a lousy time."

"Stop it!" Melissa said. "Now get up and walk around and smile. Go talk to Leo. He's around here someplace."

"I'm not interested in Leo. I keep telling you."

"Okay. Okay. So why don't you go talk to Fred Katz."

37

"I don't want to talk to Fred Katz."

"Well, talk to Sally Wong."

"She's talking to Fred Katz."

"Well, how about . . ."

A voice near my right ear said, "Imo, do you want to dance?"

I snapped my head around hopefully, but it was only Leo Hassan.

"Hi, Leo," Melissa said in her phony, sweet voice, which I hate.

Leo is Jeff's friend, and Melissa has been nagging me to go out with him for ages. She says he likes me. She says he thinks I'm pretty and smart, and she says he's a great guy. She says he's funny and intelligent and very talented. He's talented all right, and that's the chief reason I'm not interested in him. It's his voice. It hasn't changed yet, and when he sings he's a soprano. Mrs. Powers is crazy about his voice. She's cast him to sing the part of the sorceress in *Dido and Aeneas* by Purcell at a special performance in May. He certainly is talented, but how can you like a guy whose voice is higher than your own?

I got up anyway, and started dancing with him. Leo is very tall and thin, built, I'd say, like an upside-down scallion. He's got a round, smooth face and messy hair. The only good thing about dancing with him is that I don't have to stoop.

"So how are things, Imo?" Leo asked, bobbing his head up and down on his long, thin neck.

"Oh just great. Just great," I mumbled.

Leo snapped his fingers in the air, and whirled around, bumping into Rodney and Brenda.

38

"Hey Leo," Rodney said, laughing, "watch those dancing feet. Hi there, Imo. Haven't had a chance to talk to you tonight. How are you, Imo?" His voice dripped with fake concern. "Having a good time?" Pig Face, I thought. Bead Eyes. Bone Head.

"Just great, Rodney," I said, shaking my hips, and turning my back on him. I smiled up into Leo's face, and pretended to be enjoying myself. We lurched around a little while longer, and then I said, "Leo, I don't feel like dancing anymore."

"Neither do I," Leo said. "Let's get something to eat."

I didn't want to hang out with Leo, but he pulled me along with him to the food. Jeff and Melissa joined us there as Leo began piling salami, cheese, pickles and pretzels onto a big hunk of French bread.

"The food's really gross here," Jeff said. "Why don't we go get something decent."

"Okay." Leo stuffed the big open-faced sandwich into his mouth. "Just let me finish this."

Melissa burst out laughing.

"What's so funny?" Jeff asked. He is older than the rest of us—sixteen and a junior, while Melissa, Leo and I are sophomores.

"Oh, it's nothing," Melissa said, trying not to look at Leo as he stuffed some more salami, cheese and pretzels into his mouth.

"Well, what do you say?" Jeff demanded. "We could get some spinakopita over at Stoyanoff's. They're open late on Saturdays."

Jeff is into ethnic foods and yuppie life-styles. He is a very good-looking guy and a nice guy, even if he does try to act cool and superior. Melissa says that ever since he got his license he's been trying to behave like he's twenty-one.

Leo picked up some fried onion rings and added them to his sandwich. "Fine with me," he said. "I'm nearly finished."

Melissa burst out laughing again.

"What do you keep laughing about?" Jeff asked, but he didn't wait for an answer. "And Leo, if you keep eating all that junk you won't be able to eat anything at Stoyanoff's."

"Oh yes, I will," Leo said, adding a dollop of potato salad to what was left of his sandwich.

And he was right. He was able to eat more than any of the rest of us. Melissa kept laughing and Jeff kept asking her why she was laughing. At first, I thought she was laughing at Leo, and that she was being mean, but after a while she seemed to be laughing for no reason at all. When Jeff tried to order wine and the waitress carded him, Melissa just about cracked up.

"What is the matter with you tonight?" Jeff demanded. "Why do you keep laughing like that?"

"Oh, it's nothing," Melissa said. "I'm just feeling good. Don't mind me."

"Why shouldn't she laugh," Leo said in his high, quavery voice. "She's better off laughing than crying. Are you going to finish that?" He pointed to a small piece of spinakopita on Jeff's plate.

"No, I'm not," Jeff said. "It's not up to par tonight. I think the oil might be a little off."

Melissa giggled.

40

"What is the matter with you?" Jeff said angrily.

Leo pulled Jeff's plate over in front of him. "Laughter is healthy," Leo said. "People who don't laugh have twice as much chance of becoming seriously sick." He put the piece of spinakopita in his mouth.

"I don't believe that," Jeff said.

"Neither do I," I said, checking my watch and wondering when I could go home.

"Oh, it's a known fact," Leo said, nodding his head. "I just read a book about a man who had an incurable disease, and he said the doctors gave him up. But he started watching funny movies and reading funny books, and laughing a lot. And he got better. Just by laughing."

Melissa started laughing again, and Leo smiled at her encouragingly.

"I don't know, Leo," Jeff said. "Sometimes you really sound like a prize jerk."

I thought so too, but I only yawned and said I thought I'd be running along. I told them there was no reason for the three of them to rush off. The restaurant was only a few blocks from my house, and I didn't mind walking. I had to get up early the next day, I said, and why didn't I just leave my share of the bill?

"I'll go too," Leo said.

"Oh, no," I told him. "Don't leave because of me." The last thing I wanted was Leo walking me home.

"That's okay," he said, getting up. "I don't mind."

I could see Melissa and Jeff exchange a quick look, and I said, "Look Leo, it's real nice of you, but I know it's out of your way, and there's absolutely no reason

41

why you should bother. I'm used to walking home by myself. I like walking home by myself."

"It's no bother at all," he said. "Come on, Imo. I want to ask you something anyway."

No, I was thinking to myself. No! If he asks me to do something with him, I'll just say no. I can say it nicely, but I'll say no.

"I'm very sorry, Leo, but it just happens I'm baby-sitting that night, and the next night, too. As a matter of fact, I'm going to be doing a lot of baby-sitting in the next month or two, and I just won't have a moment free."

I began walking quickly, but Leo who is very tall, had no trouble keeping up with me.

"Imo," he said, "I need to ask you something."

"You sang that solo beautifully tonight," I said to him.

"Did you think so? I thought I was a little flat."

"No, no. You weren't. Or if you were, nobody noticed, I'm sure. But I did think Debby King was a little off-key. . . ." I chattered on and on as we hurried along. Leo listened patiently to everything I said, and I tried to fill up every racing moment with something inconsequential. I had just paused to take a breath when Leo said quickly, "What I wanted to ask you, Imo, is what do you think I should buy for Melissa's birthday?"

"What?"

"Her birthday. Isn't she going to be fifteen in March?"

"Well yes, but you don't have to buy her a present.

It's not like you're related to her or she's your girlfriend. I'm sure she doesn't expect anything from you."

"She's my friend," Leo said in his high voice. "Being at Carrie's party tonight reminded me. I really want to get Melissa something for her birthday. She's a friend —a good friend. I can talk to her. She's very patient. She listens to me and gives me advice when I need it."

I had a pretty good idea what kind of advice she was giving him, so I said quickly, "You could always get her jewelry. She loves pink, and she's knitting herself a new pink sweater. Maybe some of those big wooden necklaces in pink."

"I don't want to get her jewelry. How about a book?"

"A book?" I said doubtfully. "She's not much of a reader."

"But you are, aren't you?" Leo said. "I know you like to read. Melissa keeps telling me that you're a big reader, and that we have a lot in common. . . ."

"Or maybe you could get her a scarf," I cried, speeding up. "She loves scarves. Or maybe a record. It's easy to get gifts for girls. She likes plants too. You could get her a plant. . . ." I didn't give him a chance to get a word in edgewise until we reached my house. I raced up the outer stairs and he hurried after me, stumbling on the last step.

"Imo," he said breathlessly, "listen, Imo. There's something else I want to ask you. Maybe we . . ."

"Just watch your step there, Leo," I said. "Something is loose on that step, so be careful going down. Make sure you don't trip, and thanks for walking me home. Good night! Good night!"

43

I quickly turned the key in the lock, and rushed inside.

"Well?" Melissa asked over the phone the next day.
"Well what?"
"What did you think of him?"
"Of whom?"
"Come on, Imo. You know I mean Leo. Isn't he a kick?" She began laughing. "I just feel so good around him. Isn't he great?"
"He's a clown," I said. "A big, clumsy clown, with a silly, squeaky voice. Just get off my back about him, Melissa. I'm not so desperate that I have to settle for somebody like Leo Hassan."
"But, Imo," Melissa said, "he's a great guy. And so bright. Just give him a chance."
"Why don't we change the subject, Melissa," I said.

Chapter 5 ❧

I had to ring Adam's doorbell twice before he answered. When he opened the door, I was surprised at how flushed and rumpled he looked.

"It's eight o'clock," I told him. "Isn't that the time you wanted me to come?"

"Oh—yeah—right—Imo," he said, looking upstairs. "I—uh—wanted to get Benjamin off to sleep before you came . . . so . . . come on up."

I followed him up the stairs into the living room. A very blonde, very pink woman, also flushed and rumpled, was sitting there holding a glass.

Adam introduced us. "This is Imo, Renee. She's sitting for me tonight."

"Hello, there, Imo," Renee said.

"Hello, there, Renee," I said back.

"So . . ." Adam said, "I don't think Benjamin will give

45

you any trouble. Once he's off, he's off. He never wakes up. But if he does, there's a bottle in the fridge. Why don't you come with me. I'll show you where everything is."

He led me into the kitchen, which was incredibly clean, with a refrigerator packed with food.

"Help yourself," Adam said. "Make yourself at home. Eat anything you like. And make sure to check out the VCR movies. I've got a whole bunch on the shelf under the TV."

We walked back into the living room. Renee was still fixed on the couch, sipping her drink.

"I don't know how to use a VCR," I told Adam.

"Well, here, let me show you."

Renee suddenly stood up. "We're late, Adam," she said. "We have to go."

"It's okay," I said. "I need to work on a report for school."

"No," Adam said firmly. "I want her to see how it works. It will only take a few minutes, Renee."

"Okay, Adam," Renee said meekly. "I need to go to the little girls' room anyway."

Adam demonstrated the VCR and then pointed out the movie tapes he had. One of them was *Star Wars*.

"I never saw *Star Wars*," I told him. "Is it good?"

"Are you kidding?" Adam looked at me and shook his head. "How could you grow up to be fourteen years old without seeing *Star Wars*?"

We were both squatting close together in front of his TV set. I could smell some kind of after-shave lotion or male cologne or just an unfamiliar smell that neither my father nor my three former boyfriends exuded. I moved away slightly, and said, "I'm almost fifteen, and it was easy."

"Well, I was just kidding," Adam said, reaching over to give me a friendly pat on my arm. "I guess I'm just a science fiction nut, and I own *Star Wars* and *The Empire Strikes Back*. I never get tired of watching them. So why don't you give yourself a treat tonight, Imo, and watch."

I stood up and said stiffly, "I've got to get my work done."

He stood up too and asked politely, "What's your report on?"

Adam Derman is a tall man—well over six feet. I had to look up into his face, and I noticed that his eyes were a smoky blue gray color.

"Oh—it's a comparison of the use of child labor in this country before and after the First World War."

"Heavy!" Adam said, shaking his head.

"Not for me," I told him. "I find the subject very interesting."

"Watch *Star Wars*," he said, smiling. "Listen to your old Uncle Adam."

Renee reappeared in the doorway, much less rumpled looking. "Let's go, Adam," she said. "We're really late."

I could hear them laughing softly together as they moved down the stairs. Creepy woman, I thought to myself as I began unpacking my books. There was soft, soupy music playing on the stereo, and I moved over and snapped it off. Then I stood there, in Adam's living room, and looked around me.

Everything was neat and tidy. The walls were white,

47

and a big, bright blue carpet covered the floor. The furniture consisted of a beige tweed sectional sofa that curved around one side of the room, a huge white coffee table, a couple of lamps, the stereo, TV, and a single, large, splashy red and blue painting over on one wall. What did the rest of the place look like, I wondered. I'd seen the kitchen—also very clean and neat, with new fixtures and bright lights. Carefully, I began exploring. The bathroom had been painted pale blue, and a painting of a very pink, very nude mermaid hung on one wall. Everything in the bathroom was as clean as everywhere else, which made me determined to clean up my own bathroom before Adam Derman ever had occasion to use it.

Framed posters of various sports events lined the walls of the hall. Down at the end were the bedrooms. In the smaller one, a soft night-light illuminated a crib. I flipped on the light in the other one, and stood looking inside, feeling guilty. But why should I feel guilty? Nobody was there. And anyway, wasn't it the responsibility of a sitter to check the place out? Wasn't it important to know where the fire escape was (in the other bedroom) for instance?

There was only one piece of furniture in the bedroom. A water bed covered with an Indian-type blanket. I didn't know anybody who had a water bed. Go on, try it! something said inside my head. No, no, that's not right! something else said. I moved a little closer. Try it! No, no! Try it! No, no! Carefully, I crouched down and put my hand on it. It moved. I sprang up and hurried out of the room. Then I hurried back and turned off the light.

I tried to work on my report, but it wasn't due for another couple of weeks and I couldn't get in the mood. Go and eat something, I thought. He told you to help yourself. But what? There were so many choices in that stocked refrigerator, that for a while, I just stood there, leaning against the door confused. Meat. Lots and lots of meat. A roast beef, two uncooked steaks, pork chops, a whole salami, a few chicken legs . . . Finally, I took a chicken leg and poured myself a Diet Coke. The chicken leg was crunchy and delicious, and I decided maybe I would watch *Star Wars*.

But I wasn't able to watch it for very long. Darth Vader had just made an entrance when I heard a little whimper over near the doorway. Benjamin stood there, watching me with the same kind of horror I had been watching Darth Vader with.

"Hey, Benjamin," I said in a friendly voice, "I'm Imo. Do you want to come over here and watch TV with me?"

Benjamin, who seemed to be about a year and a half, shook his head, which was just as well since Darth Vader was snapping the neck of his present victim. I turned off the movie, and smiled at Benjamin, who was clutching the wall.

"How about a bottle?" I asked him.

Benjamin shook his head.

"I'm Imo," I said. "I'm a friend of your daddy's."

Benjamin shook his head.

"He's going to be back soon, and he said I should stay here with you until he gets back. Do you want me to change your diaper?"

Benjamin looked around the room and he looked at

me. Then he began crying, very softly, very desperately.

Poor kid, I thought. His parents are divorced, and he's probably never been here before, and he doesn't know who I am. But I knew that this wasn't the time to get too close to him. Not yet. Not until he stopped thinking of me as Darth Vader.

"I can wiggle my ears," I told him. "Do you want to see?"

Benjamin shook his head and went on crying.

"Most people can't wiggle their ears," I told him. "And I don't do this for just anybody, but I'll do it for you if you ask me."

I sat down on the floor, not so close to frighten him but close enough for him to see me.

Benjamin kept on crying.

"Even if you don't ask me, I'll do it. Because I like you. Now you watch." I brushed my hair up from my ears, and I began wiggling them.

Benjamin stopped crying.

"I can also curl my tongue," I told him. "You watch." I stuck my tongue out and curled it. "Not everybody can curl his or her tongue either. It's a genetic thing. Now you watch me one more time, and then you can try to do it."

Benjamin shook his head.

"You don't want to try it?"

Benjamin pointed to his ears.

"You want me to wiggle my ears. Good boy!"

I wiggled my ears. And then I wiggled them again. And again. After a while, Benjamin came closer, and

50

then he came even closer. I wiggled my ears so many times, my jaw ached. But by and by Benjamin let me change his diaper, accepted a bottle, and curled up in my lap on the sofa.

"Your father is a jerk," I murmured above the slurping noises he made as he drank his milk. "Instead of staying home with you and fulfilling his obligations as a part-time father, he has to go out gallivanting with that birdbrain, Renee."

Benjamin stopped slurping to smile at me. "Well, never mind, little Benjamin," I told him. "You've got a friend."

Benjamin pointed to my ears.

We were both there, together, when Adam returned with Renee.

"What's he doing up?" she asked. I ignored her.

"He just got up and wouldn't go back to sleep," I told Adam. "I guess he was waiting for you to come home."

"Well, here I am, big fellow," Adam said, bending over Benjamin. "Come and give Daddy a big hug."

But Benjamin put his arms around my neck and laid his head down on my shoulder.

"He likes you," Adam said, beaming at the two of us.

"I've got to get out of these shoes," Renee said. Then she moved out of the room. I could hear her heels tapping on the floor. I wondered if she was on her way to the water bed, and I looked away from Adam when he said, "I'm sorry, Imo. He really never wakes up when he goes to sleep. At least—he never used to. I hope he hasn't been a pain in the neck."

"Oh no!" I protested. "He's a sweetie."

51

Benjamin raised his head and pointed to my ears.

"Why is he doing that?" Adam asked. He settled down on the couch next to me.

"Oh, he wants me to wiggle my ears." I was feeling very embarrassed all of a sudden. "Okay, Benjamin. One more time and that's it for tonight."

"Hey!" said Adam. "Just look at those ears go. You really are some kid!"

"My mother can wiggle her ears too. And so can one of her aunts and two of her cousins. It runs in her family the same way tongue curling does on my father's side. . . ."

I was jabbering away, which I always do when I'm embarrassed. Adam laughed and reached across me to pick up Benjamin. "Now kiss Imo good night, Benjamin," he said. "She has to go home, but she'll be here next time you come."

"Sure thing, Benjamín," I said, and waved at him as his father carried him off to bed.

I had my books all packed and was sitting there awkwardly, wondering if I should hang around and wait to be paid, or if I should leave and let him pay me the next time he saw me. I could hear the sounds of somebody taking a shower, and I decided to leave.

But Adam returned just as I was about to move down the stairs.

"Here, Imo, let me pay you," he said. "I'm really sorry Benjamin got up. I guess you didn't get much of your schoolwork done."

"I was watching *Star Wars,*" I told him.

"No kidding! How far did you get?"

"Only to the part where Darth Vader raises that guy off the floor and breaks his neck."

"Oh, you haven't seen anything yet. But, Imo, if you want to come up any other time, you can. You don't have to wait until you baby-sit."

"Well thanks, but . . ."

"As a matter of fact, you can even come up if I'm not here. Your grandmother has the key." He thought for a moment, and then he said, "But maybe you'd better let me know first."

I thought of the water bed, and I said quickly, "I ate a piece of the chicken. It was delicious. Did you make it?"

"No," he said. "Renee did. I'm not a bad short-order cook—you know—steaks and baked potatoes. But I'm not much on real cooking. Not like the lady downstairs."

"Which lady?"

"I don't remember her name. It's not your grandmother." He shook his head vigorously. "It's the one in the apartment under mine. Sometimes when I come home, I can smell all those great smells coming out of her apartment. She must be some cook."

"Oh, you mean Mrs. Sloane. She lives down below you. Yes, she is a great cook."

"I like good cooking," Adam said.

"I do too," I said and then wondered why I'd said it.

"Well . . ." Adam held out fifteen dollars. I argued that it was too much, but he insisted that I take it. "I want you to sit for me whenever Benjamin comes over —probably every weekend. I'll work my schedule around yours," he said as he walked me to the stairs. "I can see that you're great with kids, and I want him to be happy. I feel very lucky that you live here."

"Adam!" Renee yelled.

"In a minute," he said. I told him he didn't have to walk me downstairs for me to go back upstairs on my side of the building. But he insisted. And he patted my shoulder, and thanked me again before I said goodnight.

Chapter 6 ❧

I've always liked boys. Even when I was twelve or thirteen, I liked boys. Not the silly, giggly way some girls do. That's not my style. Maybe if I were short and small-boned, I might have turned out that way, but it's impossible to act cutesie when you're nearly five feet ten and wear a size 9 shoe.

But I like boys. I think about them a lot, and I find just about all of them attractive. Nearly all of them. Leo Hassan is an exception. What worries me is that I don't seem to be able to focus on one boy at a time. Even when I was going around with Rodney, I still couldn't help noticing how cute Danny Petersen was. He sings bass in our chorus, and I knew I'd never get to stand next to him. Our romance was doomed even before it began, but I thought about him anyway.

He wasn't the only one either. For instance, I

couldn't help watching the head of a boy in front of me on the bus one day, and daydreaming that he would turn around, ask me if I knew where Sears was, and I would say sure, and then he would laugh, and I would smile, and his teeth would be even and white and gleaming. . . .

I'm always daydreaming, and lots of times I'm ashamed of what's going on in my daydreams. Sometimes I can be daydreaming about a couple of boys at the same time. It's disgusting.

Mark Feller, the boy in the allergist's office, was already there when I came into the waiting room. I noticed that he was reading a book, and I tried not to look in his direction as I greeted Mr. Helling and Mrs. Foster. They smiled and nodded at me, but both of them were deep in a conversation about Mrs. Foster's eczema and Mr. Helling's asthma, and both were speaking at the same time.

I picked up a magazine, and tried to struggle against it. But it was no use, and I felt myself slipping. . . .

Mark Feller looks up and smiles. "I love to read," he says.

"Yes," I tell him. "So do I. What book do you have there?"

"It's Jane Eyre," he says. "It's a wonderful book."

"It's my favorite," I say.

"Yes, I think it will be mine too." His voice is deep and resonant. "I admire the heroine. She's not a silly, giggly girl like so many girls. She's deep and serious and strong."

56

"But many boys prefer the other kind of girl," I murmur.

"Only the foolish ones," he says, looking at me with a clear, steady gaze that I meet with a clear, steady gaze of my own.

"Do you read a lot?" I ask him.

"Yes. Do you?"

"Yes."

"I can see we have a lot in common," he says. Then he smiles, gets up, sits down next to me, and asks me my name.

Mark Feller looked up and sneezed. Then he sneezed again, looked helplessly around the room, and ducked down behind his book from where we all could hear another muffled sneeze.

"Cats," Mr. Helling wheezed in sympathy. "Somebody has been here who has cats. I felt it as soon as I stepped in here this afternoon."

My grandmother's door was closed, I noticed, when I got home, and I rang the bell and yelled, "Lin Lin, are you home?" Nobody answered.

"Lin Lin's door is closed," I told my father who had about twenty photographs hanging up on one wall of his room.

"Come over here, Imo, and tell me what you think of these shots."

I stood in front of them and looked. Each of them showed the same hill covered with blue lupine and orange California poppies.

"They're beautiful, Dad, but all of them look the same to me."

"Look again," said my father.

I looked. "Oh yes, I see," I said, pointing to one of the photos. "There are two tiny figures over here in this one."

"Uh huh," said my father. "Anything else?"

"Oh yes," I said, beginning to catch on. "Over here in this one, you can see a piece of a freeway, and—oh, look—this one has a huge gray cloud. . . ."

"Yes, yes," said my father. "It's the same hill, but each time I shot it, I added something else."

"It's like that song we always used to sing," I said. "You know, about the hole in the middle of the sea. And then suddenly there's a frog in the hole in the middle of the sea, and a fly on the frog in the hole in the middle of the sea—and on and on. Oh Dad, what a wonderful idea. I love it."

"Well, it's not exactly original," said my father modestly, "but . . ."

"It's fascinating, Dad, and I love it, but Lin Lin's door is closed, and I don't think she's home. Her car's not outside."

"She's not home," said my father. "She's at her aerobics class."

"She never closes her door. I'd better go down, and see if something's wrong."

I could hear somebody moving around as I unlocked the door to her apartment. "Lin Lin?" I shouted.

Nobody answered.

I hurried through the hall into the kitchen. A man stood there in a white uniform, holding a flashlight.

"Who are you?" I demanded.

"The exterminator," he said, kneeling down and shining his flashlight under the sink.

"I didn't know she was expecting the exterminator," I said.

The man clicked his tongue as he shone his flashlight around the floor. "Lots of ants," he said. "And earwigs. It's a big problem."

I noticed on the back of his uniform the words Acme Exterminators and that he had a large white sack of tools standing on the floor. The drawers of my grandmother's kitchen cabinets were all pulled out and the doors opened. "Have they gotten inside her dishes and silverware?" I asked.

"They've gotten in everywhere," the man said, standing up. "I can't handle this by myself. I'll have to come back tomorrow with help."

The exterminator was a very small, thin man, I noticed, but he had a big, friendly smile.

"We had ants in the shower," I said, "but they're gone now. My mother did say she saw some in the hall closet. Maybe you'd better take a look while you're here."

The exterminator looked at his watch. "I have to go to Laurel Village," he said. "Right away."

"It will only take a couple of minutes," I urged. "Here, I'll help you carry up your tools."

"No, no!" he said, grabbing his sack. "I'll come back tomorrow or better yet, later today. It's a real emergency over there. I can't waste a minute." He smiled and nodded. "But don't worry. I promise I'll come back later tonight."

"Oh, I'm not exactly worried," I told him as I followed him back through the hall, thinking to myself what a nice man he was to care so much about his clients. "And you really don't have to come back tonight. I'll tell my grandmother you were here and you'll be back tomorrow."

"You do that," he said. "And have a nice day."

He was just about through the door when the top of his tool sack slipped back a little to reveal my grandmother's silver tray, which she and my grandfather had received on their 25th wedding anniversary.

"Aaah!" I yelled, realizing that he wasn't an exterminator at all but a thief who had taken advantage of Lin Lin's open-door policy.

He certainly could run very fast for such a small man, but he was carrying the heavy sack. I caught up with him halfway down the block, tackled him, knocked him down, sat on him and began yelling, "Help! Help! Help!"

"Help! Help! Help!" yelled the thief from underneath me.

"Help! Help! Help!" I continued shouting until Mrs. Uchida came flying across the street with her mop, and Mr. Kahn from his garage with a jack. Soon a bunch of other neighbors joined us.

"Help! Help! Help!" the thief continued yelling.

"Why are *you* yelling 'Help'?" I asked him, looking down at his little, red face, which wasn't smiling anymore.

"You're crushing me," he yelled. "that's why I'm yelling. Get off me. Help!"

Adam Derman drove up just as the police arrived. He

stood there listening as the officers praised me for my courage and told me they thought the thief was probably Jackson Pullitzer, the most wanted housebreaker in the area, who always disguised himself as either an exterminator, a telephone installer or an inspector from the fire department.

After they took him away, the neighbors stood around for a while, talking about how nobody's house was safe anymore and how you shouldn't open the door to anyone.

"My grandmother never keeps her door closed," I told them. "Maybe now she will."

Mrs. Uchida said that she didn't think it made any difference at all whether you locked your doors or not. She said that she was robbed only six or seven months ago when she and Mr. Uchida went out one rainy afternoon to a bargain matinee. They had locked all their doors and downstairs windows, but the thief came in over the roof and in through the upstairs bathroom window. He had taken all her jewelry and only the best silver.

Some of the other neighbors offered other stories, but Adam Derman remained silent until everybody had dispersed. He was wearing jeans and an old jacket, so I knew he was coming home from the garage where he worked.

He took me by the elbow and began walking back with me to our building.

"Would you tell me how you knew there was somebody in your grandmother's apartment?" he asked. "I missed that part."

"Well, I noticed her door was closed. You see, my

61

grandmother never closes her door. So I went upstairs and told my father."

"Good," he said. "You told your father, and what did he say?"

"Well, he was busy, so I said I thought I'd better have a look, and I got her key."

"Now, just wait a minute!" Adam said gravely. "You told your father you thought something was wrong, and he let you go down by yourself?"

"Oh, he probably didn't even hear what I was saying. He was busy with his hill photos."

"His what?"

"His hill photos. He's a photographer. So anyway, I went downstairs, and I saw him. Only I thought he was the exterminator until I noticed my grandmother's silver tray in his sack. Then I knew he wasn't the exterminator."

"Go on!" Adam said grimly.

"Well—so then I chased him down the street, and—you saw—the neighbors came and somebody called the police."

"But Imo . . ." Adam stopped walking, and turned me around to face him. "Imo, that was a very dangerous thing you did."

"Dangerous?"

"Yes. Don't you realize this man is a professional housebreaker? He could have been carrying a gun or a knife. He's a dangerous criminal."

"He was a little guy," I said weakly, "but he could run pretty fast."

"Imo, Imo!" said Adam, shaking me a little bit. "You're really a remarkable girl, and it's a wonderful thing that you're so brave. But you mustn't be foolish. You mustn't ever let this kind of thing happen again. You should have called for help. You should have called your father. You took a very foolish chance getting so close to such a dangerous criminal. You could have been hurt very badly."

"I nearly crushed him," I said, looking up into Adam Derman's smoky blue gray eyes, and feeling his strong hands on my shoulders. How tall he was, and how small I suddenly felt, wonderfully small and wonderfully delicate. I felt a delicious little shiver run from my neck all the way down to my toes.

"I know your father is going to be very upset when he hears what happened. He's going to feel terrible that he let you go downstairs by yourself. And your mother . . ." Adam shook his head. "I hate to think what your poor mother will say."

I began sneezing.

"And you're cold," Adam said, putting a warm arm around me. "You're wearing only a thin blouse."

I sneezed again, and my nose started running.

"Come on now. I'll help you upstairs," he said, moving me toward our house.

"No, no," I told him. "It's just my allergies." I wanted to laugh and cry at the same time. Here, this tall, strong, wonderful man was holding me tight, and I had to get away from him so I could blow my nose.

I persuaded him not to come upstairs with me, and I sneezed my way into our apartment and buried my nose in a clump of tissues.

My father was still in his room, studying the photos. "There was a thief downstairs in Lin Lin's apart-

63

ment," I told him between sneezes. "He said he was the exterminator, but he had Lin Lin's 25th anniversary tray in his sack. So I caught him, and the police just took him away." I sneezed a few more times, and my father turned to look at me.

"You sound terrible, Imo," he said. "Are you all right?"

"Oh sure, I'm all right." I said. "He was a little guy—the thief, I mean—and I sat on him until the police came. But Adam Derman said I should have called you. He said it was a very dangerous thing I did." The delicious shiver started running again, and I sneezed a few more times.

"Yes, it *was* dangerous," said my father gravely. "He's right. You should have called me. Why didn't you?"

"Because there wasn't time. He could run pretty fast, and if I waited to call you he would have gotten away."

My father was listening to me with a very serious look on his face. He began shaking his head, and then he said proudly, "What a daughter I have! Not only is she smart and beautiful, but she's brave as well."

"Oh Dad," I said, "I'm not beautiful."

"And strong, too," said my father, beginning to smile. "Did you actually sit on him until the police came?"

"Yes, I did. But Adam said . . ."

My father burst out laughing. "Oh wait until your mother hears this. She'll be so proud."

"Adam said she'd be upset."

"Of course she'll be upset," said my father, wiping his eyes. "She'll wish she could have been there to see it. And so do I. I could have gotten some marvelous pictures. But we can't have everything. Now start all over again from the beginning. Don't leave anything out. I want to hear the whole story."

When my mother arrived home from school, I had to go through it all over again, and she was every bit as proud as my father. They both insisted that we go out for dinner to celebrate. I had a good time that night, but I didn't forget about Adam Derman.

Chapter 7 ❧

The next day, my mother and father each spoke to Lin Lin separately about keeping her door closed.

"I tried to sound very solemn," said my mother, twisting her face into a make-believe grim mask, "and I just hope it does some good."

"She never listens to me," I said.

My mother assumed her usual cheerful face. "She just finds it impossible to believe that there's anybody bad out there in the world. She thinks everybody's the way she is."

"She's childish," I said severely. "Don't you think Lin Lin's childish?"

My mother was sitting over her books at the desk in her bedroom. I was lying across my parents' bed, and I watched her screw up her face thoughtfully.

"Childish?" my mother repeated.

"Yes, childish. It's childish and irresponsible to behave the way Lin Lin behaves."

"I suppose she is unusual," said my mother, "but I wouldn't say she was childish. She marches to a different drummer is what I'd say. But she's good and kind and happy, too. Isn't that what's important, Imo?"

I didn't answer. My mother watched me for a moment or two, then she picked up one of her books. "Do you have any homework, Imo?" she asked. Which meant that she did. But there were some things on my mind that I needed to talk to her about.

"Can I ask you something, Mom?"

"What is it, dear?" My mother put down her book.

"Well, I wondered, when you first married Dad, didn't you think he was going to work at something?"

"But he did work at something. In those days he did the most beautiful portraits of people. He liked to take them outside in natural light. And if the subject was a woman or a child, he liked them to wear flowers in their hair or carry flowers. Sometimes, he brought them the flowers himself, and once he even brought a wonderful white orchid for a dark-haired Greek girl. It was a magnificent picture but the orchid was expensive, and I think it cost him maybe twice as much as what she paid for the portrait."

"You see—that's just what I mean, Mom. When you married Dad, didn't you think he was going to make a living?"

My mother looked puzzled. "But Imo, you know talented people often don't make a living."

"All right then, didn't you think you were going to have to make a living."

67

"I certainly did." My mother nodded. "That's why I decided to go to graduate school. So that I could get an education first."

"But Mom, you've never left school. You've never worked for a living. Neither has Dad. Neither has Lin Lin. You've all just lived off *The Friendship Cookbook*. But now the royalties are really diminishing. I'll be glad if we have enough just to pay our bills this year."

"The same thing happened when wheat germ came in," said my mother thoughtfully. "Everybody wanted to buy those healthy cookbooks, and for a while your grandfather—he was such a wonderful man, Imo, a lot like you—anyway, he got a little nervous and thought he might have to go back to gardening. We all were upset. But it passed." My mother laughed. "For a few years, the royalties weren't so good, but then I guess people realized all those healthy recipes didn't taste good and started buying *The Friendship Cookbook* again." She patted my hand. "I wouldn't worry if I were you, Imo. We've lived through other times like that, and things always improved." She picked up her book again.

"Okay, Mom, can I ask you something else?"

"Of course, dear." She put her book down again, got up from her seat, and sat down next to me on the bed. "You're full of questions tonight, Imo."

"You're not too busy, are you, Mom? I know you're working on a paper."

My mother began stroking my hair. "I'm never too busy for my baby," she said. "Is everything going all right these days? You've been looking kind of down in the mouth. I hope you're not brooding over Rodney."

68

"Rodney? Oh no, Mom. But I was just thinking. Could we invite Adam for dinner one night?"

"Of course we can. It's nice of you to think of him. Poor man, living up there all by himself." My mother began twisting my hair around her fingers. "You have such lovely hair, Imo," she said. "Do you remember how you used to wear it in one long braid down your back until you were in third grade? You looked so cute. But then you said nobody else wore braids, and you wanted it cut. Your father cried when we cut your hair. Do you remember?"

"Yes, Mom, I do. But anyway, when should we invite Adam?"

"Well, let me see. Today is Thursday, and I want to get my paper finished over the weekend. How about Monday or Tuesday? I can pick up some tacos at Taco Bell on my way home that night."

"Let's make it Monday, and you don't have to pick up tacos because I'll cook."

"Oh that's nice, Imo. I'll try to catch him today or tomorrow and ask him for Monday then."

"Maybe I'll make something special," I said. "Maybe I can try out something new. I'll have time over the weekend."

"I thought that frozen Spanish rice your father fixed last week was delicious," said my mother as she picked up her book again.

On Saturday night I was sitting for Adam, and he had asked me to come at six o'clock. At five, I put on a clean white sweater, plunked myself down in front of the mirror in my room, and sorrowed as I looked at my face.

Why couldn't I have had a small rosy face like my mother's instead of my own long, sallow one? Why couldn't I have had blue eyes and a head full of blond curls like my father's instead of brown eyes and nondescript brown hair? Emphasize your best feature, said the glamour magazines. But which was my best feature? Not my long, red-tipped nose, which always ran nonstop with the advent of spring. I dabbed at it murderously. Not my full mouth, droopy now from all the sneezing I'd been doing, or my heavy-lidded eyes. I worked over all my features with eye makeup, peach glow lipstick, and powder. When I finished, I tilted my head to one side and saw—only me.

"Hey, Imo, you look great," Adam said when he opened the door. "Your secret admirer will be impressed."

"Admirer? Oh—you mean Benjamin," I said, following him up the stairs.

Little Benjamin was sitting in his high chair, in the kitchen, eating bananas and yogurt.

"Imo," he said as soon as he saw me, and pointed to my ears.

"He said Imo," I cried. "He knows my name."

"We've been practicing," Adam explained.

"But that's fantastic." I felt so happy, I wanted to pick Benjamin up, even with his face all plastered with yogurt and bananas, and give him a hug.

"And he can say something else. Can't you, big fellow?" Adam said. "Go ahead. Tell Imo what you want her to do. Go ahead."

Benjamin grinned.

"Go ahead. Don't tell me you forgot. Here, I'll whisper in your ear." Adam bent over his son, and then Benjamin looked at me. "Imo," he said. "Iggy."

"What?"

"Iggy." Adam was smiling at me, his white teeth gleaming. And little Benjamin was smiling too. I felt gloriously happy until I heard the voice.

"Adam," it called.

Adam shook his head, and said to me, "He's telling you to wiggle your ears."

"Renee's calling you." I turned away from him. "Okay, Benjamin," I said, bending over the baby, "here I go." I wiggled my ears a few times, and then Adam said, from behind me. "It's not Renee."

"What?" I stood up and faced him.

"Her name is Lori."

"Oh!"

"Iggy!" said Benjamin.

I sat down in front of Benjamin, wiggled my ears, and then made believe I was going to eat some of his banana and yogurt. "Yum, yum," I said. "I'm hungry." The baby's big eyes opened wide. Solemnly, he picked up his spoon and directed it toward my face.

I was aware that Adam was still standing behind me, but I kept my eyes on the baby's spoon as it came closer and closer to my mouth.

"Adam, how cold does it get here at night?" said the voice.

The baby's spoon hit my lips, and I made believe I was eating some of the mess. "Yum, yum," I said.

"Oh, Lori, I want you to meet Imo, Benjamin's sitter. Imo, this is Lori."

I turned. A very pretty, slim, dark-haired woman,

fastening on a pair of earrings, smiled at me from the doorway.

"Hello, Imo," she said, as Benjamin's spoon hit my ear. Lori giggled. "We've been practicing your name all day. I'm certainly glad to meet *you*."

"Gladtomeetyoutoo," I mumbled.

"Adam's been telling me about you," Lori said. "I understand you're a heroine. That you single-handedly captured a dangerous criminal."

"He wasn't so dangerous," I muttered.

"Dangerous enough," Adam said. "She'll be wiser next time, won't you, Imo? You'll make sure to call for help, right?"

"Right, Adam," I said, feeling that delicious tingle down my spine again.

"Well it sounds as if she managed pretty well on her own," Lori said. "Good for you, Imo."

"Those are funny earrings you're wearing," Adam said to Lori.

"I made them," she answered, "out of fish bones and copper wire. Most people think they're ivory."

"I think they're weird," Adam said.

"Oh, you'll get used to them." Lori waved her hand. "But tell me how cold it gets here at night. Do I need a heavy jacket?"

She and Adam discussed the temperature for a while. The baby emptied a couple of banana pieces out on his tray and was occupied for the moment in trying to mash them up with his fingers.

When Lori went off to get her jacket, Adam asked me in a low voice, "What did you think of her earrings?"

"I really didn't get a good look at them," I told him.

"I think they're gross. She has lousy taste in earrings. She always did."

"Oh!" I concentrated on the mashed bananas. "She seems very nice."

"Yes, she is," he said. "She's a friend of my sister's in Denver. I've known her for a long time, and she always wore weird earrings. She's kind of stubborn and independent, but she's not a bad kid. She's spending a few days in San Francisco on her way to Hawaii for a vacation. My sister asked me to put her up and show her around. She's sleeping in Benjamin's room."

I picked up the baby's spoon and put some yogurt on it. "Here comes the big 747," I said, swooping the spoon around. "Here it comes into the airport. Zoom! Zoom! Zoom!"

The baby laughed, and I heard Adam walk out of the room. Later, after I had given Benjamin a bath, we played together on the floor of the kitchen with pots and pans. I showed him how he could make music with two pot tops, and I sang excerpts from the "Hallelujah" chorus while he accompanied me.

After he went to sleep, I cleaned up the kitchen and decided to watch *Star Wars*. But first—I tiptoed back into Adam's bedroom. Everything was astonishingly neat and orderly, very different from the bedrooms in our apartment. There was a closet in the room, and I opened it. All of Adam's clothing hung neatly inside. His shoes, carefully polished with no worn-out heels, nestled in a shoe bag on the inside door. On a shelf above the hanging clothes, a few sweaters had been arranged in an orderly pile. The hangers hung in straight, parallel lines, so different from the hangers in

73

our closets, which converged or stuck up at odd angles. How could anybody be so neat?

I was about to close the closet when I noticed something sticking out from beneath one of the sweaters. I tugged on it and pulled out a photograph of a man, woman, and tiny baby. Adam, Benjamin, and—Benjamin's mother, Adam's former wife. There was something familiar about her face, which was strange because I had never seen her before in my life. She wore a pale blue sweater, and Adam had his arm around her shoulder. Both of them were smiling. I had to admit that she was very pretty, and that her teeth looked white and even.

I shoved the picture back under the sweaters, careful to let a little piece of it stick out. Then I closed the closet door and began moving out of the room. But I didn't. I stopped above the water bed. Try it! something said. No, don't! said something else.

I knelt down and carefully slid myself diagonally across the bed. It moved. Quickly, I jumped up, turned off the light, and hurried out of the room.

In the bathroom, I smiled at the mirror in order to see my teeth. Maybe they weren't as straight as his former wife's, but they weren't too bad. I tried to imagine myself in a pale blue sweater, and I thought one day when there was money, maybe I could buy myself one.

He comes up behind me and puts an arm around my shoulder. "Imo," he says, "I don't like those earrings."

"I'll take them off, Adam, right this minute. I'll never wear them again."

74

*"You look lovely in that pale blue sweater," he mur-
murs.*

*"I've never worn pale blue before," I tell him, smil-
ing, "but now I will. If you think I should."*

"Yes," he says. "I think you should."

"You don't think it's too much?"

*"No," he murmurs, "it's not too much, and it goes so
well with your skin."*

"I always thought my skin was sallow," I say.

*"No, my love," he says. "Your skin is the color of rare
ivory. . . ."*

The phone rang.

"Hello, hello," I cried.

"Hello," said a woman's voice. "Is Adam there?"

"No," I said, "he's not. This is the baby-sitter."

"Oh!"

"Can I take a message?" I inquired politely.

"Do you know where he went?"

"Well, no, I don't. Would you like to leave a message?"

"This is Renee," she said. "Is this—uh—is this the girl
who was sitting for him last week?"

"Yes, it is. This is Imo. Hello, Renee."

"Yeah. Hello, Imo. You're sure you don't know where
he went?"

"No, I'm sorry I don't. I'll tell him you called."

"All right. Tell him I called. And tell him he can call
me back tomorrow before noon. Wait! Tell him I'll be
home all day. He can get me anytime tomorrow. Tell
him I'll be waiting to hear from him."

"I'll tell him," I said. "Bye now."

Adam received two other calls from women friends who wanted him to call back tomorrow. I wrote everything down, and when they returned just after midnight, I gave him his messages while Lori stood there, smiling.

"Renee called," I told him. "She wants you to call her back tomorrow. She says she'll be waiting to hear from you. Frieda Langhorn called, and she wants to change the time you're getting together on Tuesday. Then you got a call from Susan Phillips, who said you should call her back as soon as you can."

"Susan Phillips?" Adam said desperately. "Susan Phillips?"

"Yes, Susan Phillips. She said to tell you that she was the short redhead you danced with at Heather Hopkins's party, about three weeks ago. You took her home. She said to remind you that you admired her cat—a white Persian with a cast in one eye and a . . ."

"I remember," Adam said.

Chapter 8 ❧

My grandmother said she didn't think there were turtles in mock turtle soup even though she couldn't remember ever having tasted it.

I borrowed her copy of *The Friendship Cookbook* and brought it upstairs. Of course, I had seen it before and even flipped through its pages from time to time. It had a picture of my great-great-aunt on the cover—a large woman in a white apron with a smile that I guess was meant to look friendly. Inside, there were funny, old-fashioned black-and-white photographs of women cooking, and at the beginning of each chapter was an appropriate quote. "The way to a man's heart is through his stomach" introduced chapter 1. Considering that my great-great-aunt never married, it seemed a curious selection.

The chapter on soups had as its quote, "Soup of the

evening, beautiful soup," and I turned the pages until I found the recipe for mock turtle soup.

"Clean and wash one calf's head, and soak one hour in cold water to cover . . ." it began.

I closed the book and decided to eliminate mock turtle soup from Monday night's menu.

This was on the Sunday before the Monday Adam Derman was coming to dinner. Unfortunately, Lori would also be coming. She wasn't due to leave for Hawaii until Wednesday morning. If I'd only known before, I could have planned the dinner for after her departure. Even though Adam said she was his sister's friend, I still didn't trust her.

But it was too late. My mother had already extended the invitation, and *he* would be coming to dinner tomorrow night. *He* would be sitting down at our dining room table, eating off our plates, and tasting food that *he* loved.

He chews slowly, his eyes closed. When he speaks, his voice is hushed and reverent. "This soup (no, no not soup!) . . . This chicken fricassee tastes exquisite—exactly the way my mother used to make it."

He turns toward Mom. "Thank you for cooking such a memorable meal.

"Oh no," Mom tells him. "I didn't cook it. Imo did."

"Imo," he says, turning toward me, "Imo, I'll never forget it . . . or you."

That's enough, I said to myself severely. Cut it out! You still don't even know what kind of things are in chicken fricassee. That word could mean anything.

Nervously, I opened to the chapter on poultry and game birds. The quote was encouraging. "And we meet again with champagne and a chicken at last." I found the recipe for chicken fricassee and read it over a couple of times.

I felt relieved. The recipe did not appear to be anything I couldn't handle. Which left only the lemon pudding. "The proof of the pudding is in the eating," said the quote at the beginning of the desserts chapter. That recipe also did not seem too frightening. I had all day to shop and cook. Both dishes could be prepared ahead of time, so that tomorrow night I would only have to make the rice and a salad.

"Don't you think we should have a bottle of wine for tomorrow night?" I asked my mother, who was typing up her report.

"Why?" my mother asked.

"Well, we are having Adam and Lori down for dinner tomorrow night."

"Do you think they drink wine?"

"I noticed wine in Adam's refrigerator, and I'm cooking chicken fricassee tomorrow night. Wine goes very nicely with chicken. Maybe champagne would be best."

"Whatever you say, dear," said my mother, crossing something out on the page in front of her.

"You'll have to pick it up or Daddy will."

"Okay. I'll get a bottle tomorrow on my way home from school."

"Please don't come home too late, Mom. The wine has to be chilled. And don't forget."

My mother turned and smiled at me. "What did you say you were making, Imo?"

"I said I was making chicken fricassee, and we'll have an old-fashioned lemon pudding for dessert."

"What an unusual menu," said my mother. "Why in the world did you pick it?"

"Because Adam said his mother used to make chicken fricassee and lemon pudding. It was on the night he came down and tasted a piece of the Friendship Cake."

"Oh yes, I remember that night. Maybe that's why he seemed a little uncertain about coming to dinner when I invited him."

"He won't be sorry," I said. "I'm making a dinner he'll really love."

I got my father to help clean the house on Sunday afternoon. It didn't look anywhere as neat as Adam's when we finished, but at least all the usual clutter had been picked up in the living room, and the bathroom fixtures had been scrubbed reasonably clean. My father also offered to help with the cooking, but I declined. I wanted to make everything all by myself. It took a long time, but by ten o'clock at night, the chicken was finished and so was the pudding.

"Mmm," said my father, coming into the kitchen, "something smells good."

"Hey, Dad," I said, "would you taste a piece of this chicken and give me your opinion?" I put a small piece of chicken on a plate, spooned some gravy over it, and handed it to my father. I watched as he put some into his mouth and began chewing.

"Well?" I demanded. "What do you think?"

My father swallowed, staggered backward, and put up a hand to his head.

80

"What is it, Dad? What happened?"

My father began gurgling. He put his hand around his throat, and sank to the floor.

"Dad, Dad!" I cried. "What's wrong, Dad?"

I bent over him. Both of his eyes were closed. Suddenly one opened. He winked at me, grinned, and said, "That's pretty good, Imo. Can I have another piece?"

Monday afternoon, I hurried home after school and began panicking. Neither of my parents was home. Even though the chicken and the pudding were cooked, it suddenly occurred to me that people usually sat around and ate hors d'oeuvres before dinner. I'd forgotten about hors d'oeuvres. And then there was the salad. Should we eat the salad before the chicken fricassee or with it or after it? And what about a tablecloth? The only clean tablecloth was the old blue-and-white checked one. But how did that look with our tan dishes? And what about a centerpiece, and why didn't I remember to buy candles yesterday when I shopped? And would my mother remember to pick up the wine? And what should I wear? And why did the rubber plant in the living room look so mangy, and was there a fresh bar of soap in the bathroom?

I was exhausted by the time everybody arrived. My mother had forgotten to buy the wine, but Adam and Lori brought a bottle. Everybody offered to help, but I wanted Adam to understand that I was doing the cooking all by myself that evening, so I told them all to go inside and enjoy themselves.

I could hear them laughing and talking as I scurried around the kitchen. Start the salad, I muttered to myself. Begin heating up the fricassee, make the rice, slice the bread, put the coffee in the coffeepot . . . oh wait . . . maybe they would prefer tea. . . .

Lori poked her nose into the kitchen. "Can't I give you a hand?" she said.

"No thank you," I told her firmly.

"It doesn't seem fair that you should be doing all the work while the rest of us are enjoying ourselves."

"I'm enjoying myself too," I said.

My father came into the kitchen. "Can't I do something, Imo?" he offered.

"Yes," I said, as a radish I was slicing for the salad fell on the floor. "Why don't you show Lori and Adam some of your photos? I'm sure they'd be interested."

Lori certainly was. After we were all settled around the dining room table, eating the fricassee, she was still talking about them. Actually, Lori wasn't eating. She was leaning toward my father and saying, "But what made you think of taking all those pictures of the same hill?"

My father wasn't eating either. He was too busy gobbling up all of Lori's interest in his shots. "Well," he said, "you know the Impressionist painters did the same kind of thing when they painted many pictures of the same object at different times of day."

"Those photographs of yours," Lori said fervently, "really stay in your mind. They're spectacular."

"Oh, I don't know," said my father happily.

"Hey," Adam cried, "this is delicious!"

"And the humor"—Lori swallowed a little piece of her chicken quickly so that she could continue talking —"the humor is so sophisticated."

"Oh . . . well . . ." my father murmured.

"This is really great," Adam continued. "This is the real thing. This is chicken fricassee."

"Imo made it," said my mother.

"You did!" Adam turned a look on me that made all the hours of hard work, panic, and indecision well worth it.

"Yes," Lori said, "it is delicious. This is certainly one talented family. But Adam, what did you think of Luke's pictures?"

"Oh . . . uh . . . Luke's pictures," Adam said, running his tongue slowly around his upper lip. "Uh, yes, they really are great shots. But do you think people will buy them?"

"Well, I wouldn't want to sell them except as a set," my father said.

"So what will you do with them?" Adam asked. I watched him eating, waiting for his plate to empty so I could offer him seconds.

"If I ever had a one-man show," said my father, "I could exhibit all of them there, but most of the shows I get into only want a few shots from each photographer."

"And you absolutely cannot split them up," Lori said. "Your whole point would be lost. They must be seen together."

"My former wife's brother was a photographer," Adam said, "but he never could make ends meet. He had to work in a deli part-time just to support himself."

I didn't like the turn the conversation was taking, so I offered the plate of fricassee around again even though Adam still had some on his plate. Adam laughed when the plate came to him, and helped himself to a

83

big portion. "I can't say no to this. You really are some kid, Imo!"

"Yes, she is," said my father, beginning to eat his chicken, and for a while everybody said nice things about the dinner.

When I brought in the pudding, Adam didn't notice it at first. He and Lori were busy arguing.

"If he was my kid, I wouldn't want him to play football," Lori was saying.

"Oh, it's not that dangerous," Adam answered. "People make too much of a fuss over sports injuries. I played in high school, and I hope he does, too. I can see he's going to be a big guy like his daddy."

"It's a dangerous sport," Lori insisted. "People can get killed playing football."

"People can get killed crossing the street."

"Baloney," Lori said. "I'm talking about football, so don't change the subject. If I had a kid, I'd never let him play. I'd tell him no, absolutely no. 'If you try to play football, I'll come and drag you off the field.' "

"You know something," Adam said. "You are one crazy woman. Everybody in this country loves football. Everybody except you."

He turned to look for confirmation from my father, who began brushing crumbs off the table. My mother asked, "Would anybody prefer tea to coffee?" Neither of my parents are at all interested in sports. Up until that evening, neither was I.

I began serving the pudding. When Adam noticed it, he forgot all about his argument with Lori.

"Don't tell me," he said, peering into the bowl, "don't tell me that's a lemon pudding."

84

"Uh huh," I said, spooning some out into a dish and passing it to Lori.

"If you don't mind, Imo," she said, "I'd like just a little taste. It looks marvelous, but I'm not much of a sweets eater."

"I sure am," Adam said, "especially if it's lemon pudding. This is absolutely one of my favorite desserts. Just pass her portion over here to me."

I got a few compliments on the pudding, and then my mother asked Lori what kind of work she did. Lori made a face. "I work for my father," she said. "He has a window blind and shade company. It's boring work."

"Well, why do you do it?" my father asked.

"I'm kind of stuck," Lori said. "My father keeps telling me he's going to retire and sell the business. He's been saying that for years, and everytime I say I want to do something else, he asks me just to wait a little longer."

"That must be terrible," said my mother, "working at something you don't like."

"Most people do," said Adam. "I'm not exactly crazy about my job either, but what choice do you have in life?"

"What would you like to do?" my father asked Lori.

"Oh, I'd love to make jewelry," Lori said. "I've been taking courses, and I make all my own jewelry. She was wearing a necklace and earrings that appeared to be made out of small fish heads.

"Did you make the jewelry you're wearing?" asked my mother. "It's fantastic."

"Oh yes," said my father. "It's really unique."

The three of them huddled toward each other, and

Adam looked at me, raised his eyebrows, and accepted a second portion of the lemon pudding.

"This is the best meal I've had in ages," he said.

Later, after the two of them had left and we were cleaning up, my father said, "Lori is a very charming person."

"Oh yes," said my mother, stacking a pile of plates in the sink. "Isn't she? And so pretty, too."

"I don't think she's so pretty," I said. "Her mouth is kind of big, and her teeth are crooked."

My mother giggled. "And do you know something?"

"What?"

"I think she likes Adam."

"I don't think so," I said. "She's just a friend of his sister's."

"I think Adam likes her," said my father.

"That's just ridiculous," I cried, putting the leftovers into the refrigerator, and slamming the refrigerator door so hard I could hear something drop inside. "They don't agree on anything. You heard. He likes football, she doesn't. She likes her earrings, he doesn't. She doesn't like desserts, and he does. . . ."

"I can tell he likes her," my father insisted. "He notices her. That's how you can tell. When you don't care about somebody, you don't notice her. You don't notice whether or not she's saying something you agree or disagree with. He notices. And I guess she notices him too."

"What a pity she has to go off to Hawaii," said my mother, leaning against the sink.

"But she's going to stop over on her way back," said my father, "so . . ."

"So . . . maybe we'd better finish doing the dishes or we'll be up all night," I said.

"There certainly are a lot of them to do," said my mother, looking around the kitchen. "But it was a very delicious meal, Imo, and once in a while I guess it's worth going to all that fuss and bother."

"Oh yes," said my father. "I think the chicken was every bit as good as that Swanson's frozen chicken pie you fixed the other night, Maryanne."

"I think Imo's was better," said my mother loyally. "And Imo dear, why don't you just let Daddy and me clean up tonight? You did all the cooking, so I think that's only right. I don't have an early morning class so I don't mind getting to bed late."

I was happy to leave them and shut myself into my bedroom where I could think about Adam and the way he said, "This is the best meal I've had in ages." Maybe *The Friendship Cookbook* was right, and the way to a man's heart *is* through his stomach.

Chapter 9 ❧

Melissa's birthday fell on a Saturday. For the past couple of years, her family had celebrated by making her a special dinner party. I was always invited along with a few other friends.

"This year," Melissa said, "I'm only having you, Jeff, and Leo."

"What time?" I asked.

"Oh, about six, but I was thinking that later the four of us could go to a movie."

"Well, I'm afraid I'm going to be tied up later," I said carefully. "I mean I'll definitely be coming to the dinner. Maybe I can even come earlier if you like, but I have to be back by eight thirty."

"Do you have a date?" Melissa asked, sounding surprised.

"No, not exactly, but I did promise my neighbor I'd sit for him."

"Oh!" Melissa said.

"Now don't be like that," I told her. "I am coming to the dinner, and maybe, if you're free, we could have a picnic in the park at lunchtime. Just the two of us. I'll make the sandwiches. How about it, Melissa?"

"I'll be busy earlier," Melissa said in a hurt voice, "but it's nice that you have the time to come for dinner."

"Well, how about Sunday then? Let's do something on Sunday. I'm free Sunday."

"I may not be," said Melissa.

Love certainly complicated matters. And I was in love. Deep, deep in love. I knew that Melissa was feeling neglected, and I felt sorry, but I just couldn't confide in her over the phone. I knew and she knew that I could have told Adam to find somebody else to sit for him on Saturday night. Maybe I could even have found somebody for him. Maybe my mother would have been willing to fill in.

But I couldn't help myself. I couldn't help wanting to see Adam and be with him every opportunity I had. Even though he would be going out on a date, I would see him before he left and after he returned. I would be in his house, surrounded by his things, caring for his child. My love welled up inside me, pushing all other feelings to one side. It was disgusting, but I couldn't help myself.

I also knew that Melissa was not one to carry grudges, and when I arrived at her house at five thirty, carrying

89

her birthday present with a big pink ribbon on it, she was all smiley.

"Happy Birthday, dear Melissa," I sang out when she opened the door, and handed her my gift.

"Ooh, thanks, Imo," she said, and immediately opened it. I had given her a set of pink beads and matching earrings. She put them on, and stood in front of the hall mirror admiring herself.

"They're really great, Imo." She gave me a hug and a kiss. "Look how well they go with my dress. Come on inside. I want my mother to see them."

My gift was admired by Melissa's family, and so was the new beige purse Jeff brought. Leo arrived a little after six, huffing and puffing, and looking his usual disheveled self.

"I'm sorry I'm late, Melissa," he said in his high, squeaky voice, "but I've been shopping for your present. Boy, is it hard picking out something for a girl!"

He handed her a plain bag. It wasn't wrapped and it didn't have any ribbon on it, but Melissa's face was full of smiles as she opened it. Inside were three pairs of loud, garish knee socks. One was red and had pictures of Betty Boop on it, another had bright green birds chasing orange worms on a purple background, and the third pair had rainbows going in all different directions.

"Ooh!" Melissa said.

Nobody else said anything. The socks were completely inappropriate for a girl like Melissa, who wore delicate colors like pink and baby blue and pale green.

"Well," Melissa's mother said finally, "aren't they . . . really . . . very unusual."

90

Jeff looked at me and raised his eyebrows.

"I love them." Melissa laughed and gave Leo a big hug. "They're adorable. Just what I wanted."

Then everybody else said something nice about the socks, and we all trooped into the dining room. Melissa had chosen lasagna and spinach salad for dinner, and German chocolate cake for dessert. By the time Melissa's mother brought in the cake, covered with fifteen candles, the time was already eight fifteen. I had to be over at Adam's by eight thirty. So as soon as Melissa had blown out her candles and everybody had sung "Happy Birthday to You," with Leo's voice hitting all the highest notes, I rose and said, "I'm afraid I have to go, Melissa. I'm sorry, but . . ."

"It's okay, Imo," Melissa said, smiling at me. "We'll save you a piece of cake. And let's get together tomorrow."

She wasn't angry anymore. Everybody else at the table seemed intent on the cake and the passing of dishes. Only Leo, I noticed, was watching me with a mournful look on his face. He half rose from his chair, but I moved too quickly for him and was out of the house before he had a chance to say anything.

I was breathless when I rang the bell to Adam's apartment. "Come on in, Imo. The door's open," he yelled.

I walked up the stairs, and found him in the hall, talking on the phone. Benjamin was lying on the floor near him, trying to pull out the eyes of a large black-and-white bear pillow.

"Imo!" Benjamin shouted when he saw me.

"That's ridiculous," Adam said into the phone. Then he smiled quickly at me and nodded.

91

I picked Benjamin up, carried him into the living room, and rolled him around on the floor.

"No," I could hear Adam say. "You're making it all up and you know it."

I began playing pattycake with Benjamin.

> Pattycake, pattycake, baker's man
> Bake me a cake just as fast as you can.

"I never said that," Adam said.

> Pat it and prick it and mark it with *B*
> And put it in the oven for Benjamin and me.

"Well, that's your problem. Good-bye!"

Benjamin was clapping his hands together and chanting, "Pattapattapatta . . ." when Adam stamped into the room. "Stupid woman!" he said.

"Uh—what happened?" I asked, pleased to see him look so unhappy.

"She's just a stupid woman." Adam sat down on the ground facing me. "I knew she wasn't a Phi Beta Kappa, but this dumb I didn't think anybody could be."

Benjamin began clapping his head between his hands and giggling.

"Who's a funny bunny?" I said, smiling at him, and watching Adam fume out of the corner of my eye.

"I told her at least two times last week that I would pick her up and take her out for dinner on Saturday night, and that later we'd go dancing. I explained very carefully that we were meeting another couple. I even called her two nights ago to say we had dinner reservations at nine, and that I'd pick her up at a quarter to. Now she tells me I said Sunday, not Saturday. She

92

knows damn well it was for today, but something better must have turned up. It just shows you how stupid she is. If she wanted to get out of going, she should have said she was sick or somebody died or she sprained her back. What a birdbrain!"

"I didn't think she seemed too intelligent," I said, taking Benjamin's hands and beginning to play Rowboat.

"Who?" Adam said.

"Renee," I told him.

"Oh, Renee's a genius compared to Linda. Her name is Linda. It's not Renee."

"Oh!" I started rowing very vigorously back and forth with Benjamin's arms. I sang,

> Row, row, row your boat,
> Gently down the stream.

"Now I'll have to cancel it with my friends." Adam looked at his watch. "I can't get anybody else on such short notice."

"Maybe you could go yourself," I suggested.

"Myself!" he said. "No thanks." He stood up and marched out of the room.

> Merrily, merrily, merrily
> Life is but a dream.

When Adam returned, he seemed to have recovered his spirits. "Well, that's that," he said, picking Benjamin up and swinging him around. "Now you and your daddy, big guy, are going to have a nice, long evening together."

I stood up. "Well, I guess . . ."

93

"Oh, and Imo, I'm really sorry this happened. I hope you didn't have to change any of your plans around. I know how busy you are."

"No, no," I said, "no problem."

"Well, I insist on paying you anyway."

"No," I cried. "I don't want you to pay me."

"I insist. Just take old Benjamin here for a second."

"No, Adam, I won't take any money."

"Oh yes you will," Adam said, handing the baby over to me, and giving me a little, playful tap on the head. I laughed a weak, helpless, little laugh, and sat down again with Benjamin in my lap. "Iggy," Benjamin said, and began pulling on my ears.

"You know, Imo, you're really wonderful with kids," Adam said. "I bet you'll have a bunch of them when you get married."

"Well thanks," I said, feeling my cheeks grow hot. "I like kids, but . . ."

"But what?"

"Well, I don't know if I'll ever get married." What a dumb thing to say, I thought. Why did I have to go ahead and say such a dumb thing?

"Why shouldn't you get married?" He was looking at me with a little smile that made my insides toss around and around. How handsome he was with the light shining on his golden brown skin.

"Well, I want to go to college, and then . . ."

"What are you going to study in college?"

"Accounting. I want to be an accountant."

"An accountant?" Adam said, his forehead wrinkling and his smile fading. "That's kind of a boring field for a girl like you. Why don't you go in for teaching? Maybe

94

nursery school teaching. It will give you experience with kids, and then later you'll know how to take care of your own."

"I like kids," I repeated foolishly, "but . . ."

"I bet you'll know how to take care of them too," Adam said. "I bet they'll be fed proper meals and won't have to sit around all day in wet diapers."

"Uh, no, I guess not," I said vaguely. Adam grabbed Benjamin away from me and began patting his back. I could see his thoughts were somewhere else.

"Nothing's more important than taking care of your own kids," Adam said. "Isn't that right, big guy? You're the most important thing in your daddy's life, aren't you? I'd feel a lot better if I knew your mother felt the same way."

I wondered if Benjamin's mother went out a lot too, but I kept my thoughts to myself.

"It's a funny thing," Adam said, "but some women would just be better off if they never had kids."

"Oh yes, you're absolutely right," I said.

"Lori, for instance," Adam said. "I don't know what kind of mother she'd make. She's got so many crazy ideas."

"Is she married?" I asked hopefully.

"Oh no! Who'd ever want to marry her? She's so argumentative. It's been nice and quiet around here since she left. I really enjoy coming home to a peaceful house." He gave a laugh that didn't sound very happy.

"Will she stay long on her way back from Hawaii?" I asked.

"Only a few days," he said. "I really don't mind. She can even stay longer if she wants. Even though she gives me a hard time, she's not really a bad kid. Actually, she's kind of fun when she's not arguing. One night when she was here, she helped me refinish an old oak chest I was working on, and then another night we went to a Thai restaurant. She likes that kind of food. It wasn't bad. Kind of delicate but not bad."

"I never tasted Thai food," I said.

"Well, I'm pretty much a meat-and-potato man," Adam said. "I like simple, down-home cooking like my mother used to make. Like you made for us the other night."

He was wearing a white sweater, opened at the neck, with a gold chain that gleamed against his brown gold skin. He leaned a little closer to me, and that smell of something minty and manly made me move back nervously. He didn't notice.

"I'm glad you enjoyed it," I murmured.

Adam was looking over my head, and thinking about other things. "Lori's different. She's not very domestic I guess, but sometimes you can't tell about a woman. Take my ex-wife, Jennifer. She's just the type of woman you'd swear would be a perfect wife and mother. She's really very sweet and gentle. Even now I have to admit she is. But as soon as Benjamin was born, she just fell apart."

"Ttt, ttt, ttt," I said, watching the baby make a grab at the gold chain around Adam's neck. I guessed he must be some kind of athlete to have such a beautiful golden tan. Maybe a swimmer or a tennis player.

"It was okay before he was born. I mean, she wasn't any kind of housekeeper, and I had to teach her how to cook. I guess her parents spoiled her. She was an only

96

child, and they waited on her hand and foot." He smiled at me. "You know, Imo, you have to make sure the same thing doesn't happen to you. You don't want to grow up to be incapable of taking on any kind of responsibility. It's a real danger with only children. Make sure it doesn't happen to you."

"I don't think there's any danger," I told him.

"Jennifer never seemed to get herself organized. After the baby was born, I'd come home from work, and the house would be a mess, and she'd never have anything cooked. I ended up cooking, and then she'd cry if I ever tried to help her pull herself together. She was like a kid herself. She never grew up. Even when I met her, I thought she was kind of childish."

"So why did you marry her?" I asked.

"For such a young girl, Imo, you're really very mature for your age. You've got a good head on your shoulders." He beamed at me, and I smiled back, although I wasn't sure exactly what I had said that was so mature.

"Well, I've learned my lesson, and it won't happen again. But she seemed so sweet and gentle when I first met her, so sort of delicate and fragile. Okay, I know you're going to say I'm sexist. Lori does. I'm not, but let's face it, guys do like that kind of woman. It's in the blood, I guess. Women like that make you feel ten feet tall." Adam shook his head. "But I'm older and a lot wiser now."

I thought of Renee and all the drippy women's voices I'd heard over the phone. But all I said was, "Look, Benjamin's asleep."

The baby's face was pressed against his father's chest. Adam bent down and gently kissed the top of his head.

Tears came to my eyes. "You must really miss him," I blubbered.

Adam grinned. "You're crying, little Imo. You're really a softie, aren't you?"

"Well, I think it's sad that he can't be with you. A child needs a father," I said, wiping my eyes. My nose began running. It never takes much to get my nose running.

"I tell you what," Adam said. "Let me put him in his crib, and then if you're not in a hurry, maybe we can have a glass of wine, and talk for a little. That is, if you want to stay. Maybe you'd rather do something else."

"Oh no," I said quickly. "I'd like to stay."

While Adam was busy with Benjamin, I quickly raced for the bathroom where I washed my face, combed my hair, put on fresh lipstick, and tried to staunch the flood from my nose. When I came out, I could hear Adam in the kitchen.

"Do you want something to eat, Imo?" he asked. "I'm starving."

"No, no," I told him. "I've already eaten."

I stood there in the kitchen watching him load up a plate with cold cuts and cheese. He pulled a bottle of wine out of his refrigerator, and took two glasses out of the cabinet. He poured one then hesitated over the other. "Oh," he said, "I was forgetting." He looked at me and the corners of his eyes crinkled as he smiled. "I was forgetting that you weren't grown up."

"I am grown up," I protested. "I'm almost fifteen."

"How about a Coke?" he said.

Chapter 10 🙢

Sunday morning, I tried to concentrate on helping my mother pay the bills, but it wasn't easy.

He bends over me to pour more Coke into my glass. "Tell me about you now, Imo," he says, straightening up and smiling. His teeth gleam white in the lamplight.

"I don't want to talk about me," I murmur. "I only want to listen to you.

"Imo, little Imo," he sighs, putting his hands on my shoulders, and slowly bringing his face closer to mine.

"As I see it," said my mother cheerfully, "we have $683 in the checking account, and our bills come to $1214. The royalty check is late, as usual, but I'm not worried.

I switched daydreams.

"Lean on me," he says softly. "Let me share your worries."

"Actually," my mother continued, "there should be another bill around here from a couple of months ago when Lin Lin took a piece of the garage door off that time she backed the car out. Oh—here it is. No—there are two of them—$278 from the carpenter and $185 from the auto mechanic."

How beautiful my daydreams were! My nose never ran in my daydreams, my love was always returned, and our bills invariably got paid on time.

"We'll have to be a little late this month." My mother shoved all the bills back into the desk drawer and stood up. "We'll have to wait until the royalty check arrives."

"I'm worried," I said to my mother. "What if it isn't enough? What if it's even less than the last one? What will we do if we don't have enough money to pay our bills?"

"We always have enough to pay our bills," said my mother.

"But Mom, isn't it possible that this time we won't? What will we do then?"

"Well," said my mother gravely, "I suppose we would just have to economize."

"How would we do that, Mom?"

My mother waved her hand impatiently. "Oh, lots of ways. I suppose we could cut down on the heat, and maybe eat two meals a day instead of three. I remember another time when money was scarce. We stopped buying napkins and used paper towels instead."

"Somebody could go to work," I suggested. "For money, I mean."

"Yes," agreed my mother, smiling, "somebody could. So you see, Imo, there's really nothing to worry about."

I called Melissa that morning, and agreed to go shopping with her.

I didn't really want to go anywhere—even with Melissa, but I had promised. I wanted to stay in my room with the door closed and think about last night. I wanted to think about how we had talked. And talked. And talked.

First he had, about Jennifer, about how he had loved her and cared for her and tried to make her happy. It made the prickles go up and down my spine to think of how he had loved Jennifer. Silly, thoughtless Jennifer. And I knew inside me that he was worth a million Jennifers, and that what he needed was a woman who was up to him, a woman who could care for him the way he had cared for Jennifer, a woman who could look after his home, care for his children, and give him what only one woman in this world could give him. There was only one woman who could ever be right for Adam Derman.

Me!

"You're looking kind of spacey today," Melissa said. "I hope you're not mooning over Rodney."

"Who?"

"Well if it isn't him, who is it?"

"I don't want to tell you. You'll laugh at me if I tell you," I said, knowing that I'd be telling her everything inside of a few minutes.

"I'm not going to laugh at you," she said. "Did I laugh when you told me you had a crush on Tim Krumgold or on Hal Burton back in sixth grade or even on Rodney. Did I?"

So I told her. She didn't laugh.

"You're crazy," she said. "He must be at least twice your age."

"He's more than that," I admitted, "but he's wonderful. I can tell he likes me too. He says I'm very mature for a girl my age and last night his date stood him up, so the two of us sat around for hours, just talking."

"What about?"

"Oh, first we talked about him and his problems. He was married to this real dippy woman. She was very immature and she never could take care of things properly. And she never cleaned the house or cooked or took care of Benjamin."

"Sounds like a great conversation," Melissa said. "You should have hung out with us. We really had a good time. We didn't go to the movies. We stayed home and played Trivial Pursuit. Not my parents. But Angie and Flora stayed home, and Hank's girlfriend, Ellen, came over—and we had two teams. Hank, Ellen, Jeff and Angie were on one side, and Leo, Flora and I were on the other. It was so much fun. Their team won, but we kept laughing and laughing. It was one of the best birthdays I ever had."

"So then I told him about my allergies and how I thought I wanted to be an accountant. But he thinks I should be a teacher. A nursery school teacher. He thinks I'm wonderful with kids. He thinks when I get married I should have lots and lots of kids. He said not

102

to worry about my allergies. He thinks I'm—he said I'm very attractive and no guy is going to care about my allergies."

"Well, haven't I told you that too? Haven't I told you that Leo . . ."

"Look, if you're going to start in again about Leo, I don't want to hear it. I have enough problems."

Melissa snorted. "Problems! You don't know what problems are. Leo's the one who has real problems."

"I know," I said. "With a voice like his, he's bound to have lots of problems."

"His mother is the worst. Here, hold my purse while I try on these pants." Melissa handed me her purse, and slipped on some baggy khaki-colored pants. She was wearing a pair of the socks Leo had given her for her birthday—the pair with the green birds, orange worms and purple background.

"I don't think those pants look good at all," I said. "That kind of style is not for you."

"I've decided to change my image," Melissa said, turning herself around in front of the mirror. "Anyway, Leo's mother is a real stinker. She makes fun of him and says she's ashamed to have a son who sings the way he does."

"I can't exactly blame her," I said, holding up a beautiful, soft blue sweater that made me think of that picture in Adam's closet of him and Jennifer. She was wearing a blue sweater a lot like the one I was holding.

"His voice is beautiful," Melissa said. "Nobody's got a voice like his. And he's so good-natured and patient with his mother. He was talking to me over the phone the other night, and she kept yelling for him to hang up.

You should have heard her voice. She sounded like a wounded rhinoceros. Are you going to try that sweater on?"

I was holding the sweater up in front of me. The color really was lovely.

"No, I don't think so."

"Why not? It's a great color for you."

"Because the royalty check hasn't arrived yet, and you know we're kind of broke this year."

"Go ahead. Try it on," Melissa urged.

I shook my head, and began to put it back on its hanger.

"Go ahead. I've been wondering what to get you for your birthday, and if you want that sweater, I'll buy it for you."

"But Melissa, my birthday isn't until May."

"It can be an early birthday present."

I was feeling very happy when I arrived home, holding my new sweater, and thinking how lucky I was to have a friend like Melissa. Somebody was standing in front of Adam's door, ringing his bell. She turned as I came up the stairs and gave me an uncertain smile.

I knew who she was immediately. I had felt as if I'd known her when I first saw her photo. She looked familiar then, and now she looked even more familiar. It was Jennifer, Adam's ex-wife.

"Do you live here?" she asked in a soft, little voice.

Of course she was dressed all in blue except for her jacket. Adam said she usually wore blue. Her eyes were blue too, but her hair was dark and her skin a soft ivory color. Where had I seen her before? Something tugged at my memory.

"Yes, I do," I said. "I live upstairs on this side of the building."

"Oh," she said, "you must be Imo. You must be the girl who baby-sits for my little boy, Benjamin. He talks about you all the time. I'm Jennifer. His mother, Jennifer Derman."

"HowdoyoudoMrs.Derman," I murmured.

"Maybe you know where they are," she said, a troubled look in her eyes. "I told Adam I'd be coming at four thirty to pick Benjamin up, but nobody's home."

"I don't know where they are," I told her.

"Oh dear!" She slumped against the door. "I'm sure I told him I'd be coming at four thirty, and my brother and his wife—they live across the park—they were expecting me at five. All of us were supposed to go over to my sister-in-law's aunt's house for dinner, and then Benjamin and I were going to sleep over. Well, it looks as if I'm going to be late, and maybe I should call them —my sister-in-law, I mean."

She was breathless by the time she finished, and I said, "You could come upstairs and use the phone in my house."

"Oh no," she said. "I wouldn't want to bother you."

"No bother at all," I said firmly, opening the door to our apartment and waving her in.

Both of my parents were at home, and after Jennifer made her phone call, my mother invited her to have a cup of coffee.

"Oh no," she said, "I wouldn't want to bother you."

She sounded like a kid with her soft, little voice and her breathless way of speaking. After my mother had persuaded her to sit down and have a cup of coffee, she relaxed and began chattering away. I kept looking out of the front window for Adam.

He and Benjamin didn't arrive home until five thirty.

"But I told you I was coming at four thirty," Jennifer said, when they came upstairs.

"No, you did not," Adam said severely. "You said you were coming at six."

"But I couldn't have," Jennifer cried. "I'm supposed to be over at Lloyd's house at five. I couldn't have said I was coming at six."

"You certainly did," Adam insisted. "I remember because I told you I was meeting a friend at seven and purposely asked you if you could come a little earlier. But you said you couldn't."

"Oh yes," Jennifer said, standing up. "Now I remember. Alice and I were supposed to have lunch with June and Shauna, but then Shauna had to go to the hospital because her brother had his appendix out, and Lloyd said I should come earlier because Wilma's aunt didn't like to stay up late. I thought I had told you, but maybe I forgot. Well, it's all right because I phoned Wilma, and I've had such a good time sitting here with Maryanne and Luke. And Imo too."

"How about a little more coffee?" my mother asked Jennifer. "And how about you, Adam? Would you have time for a cup?"

"Thank you," Adam said. "It's really very nice of you, but I am meeting a friend, and we've taken up enough of your time."

"Not at all," said my mother, holding the pot. Jennifer sat down again, and let my mother fill up her cup.

I picked Benjamin up and carried him off to the living room. As I had hoped, Adam followed me.

"Don't let her stay too long," he whispered. "She forgets herself, and Benjamin should be in bed before eight."

"Do you really have to go?" I asked, trying to sound cool.

"Yes, I do. I'm meeting a . . . a friend."

"I know," I said. "Linda."

"No, not Linda. Renee. But make sure Jennifer doesn't overstay her welcome."

Jennifer left soon after Adam, and my parents began talking about her.

"The baby looks just like her, doesn't he?" said my mother.

"I don't think so," I said. "I think he looks like his father. But what did you think of her?"

"She looks familiar," said my father, "but I can't think where I might have met her before."

"I thought so too," said my mother. "Such a pretty face. It's obvious Adam likes good-looking women."

"That's not all he likes," I said. "He likes intelligent women too, and capable women. He's not just interested in a pretty face."

"She's kind of sweet," said my father, "but . . ."

"Yes," said my mother, "I know what you mean."

Later, I went into my room, and tried on the new sweater. It was a soft, fuzzy sweater with a boat neck, and it made me look different. Not like myself. I loved it, and stood in front of the mirror, turning and twisting my head, and trying not to notice my red nose and puffy eyes.

I came out to show my parents.

"That's pretty," said my father. "You look nice in that sweater."

"You look like Jennifer," said my mother.

Chapter II ✖

Suddenly Leo's voice changed. Just a few weeks before he was to sing the part of the sorceress in *Dido and Aeneas.*

I didn't know what to say to him. It didn't even seem like Leo with his deep, new voice.

"Mrs. Powers is upset," Leo told me. "She says she's going to have to substitute Marcia Bingham, and that Marcia doesn't have the range I have—I mean I used to have."

I mumbled something about yes he did have—or used to have—a wonderful voice, and I noticed some little dark hairs sprouting on his chin.

"My mother's happy," Leo said. "I guess I finally did something she approves of."

I burst out laughing, and Leo joined in. Maybe he

really did have a good sense of humor. And he was tall
—taller than most of the boys I knew.

Mrs. Powers asked me to stay after chorus that day.
I wondered if something was wrong with my voice too.
But no, nothing was wrong. Everything was right.

"She wants me to sing a solo," I told my parents when
I got home. "Me. She wants me to sing a solo. It's for the
final concert. She says my voice is just perfect for the
part. Just think—I'm going to sing a solo."

"Well, that's wonderful." My mother grabbed me
and kissed me. Then she passed me over to my father
who grabbed and kissed me too.

"Well," I said, finally untangling myself, "it's not really a big solo. Actually, there are three of us—three
sopranos. One of them is Marcia Bingham. She's really
got a magnificent voice. And then there's Debby King
—her voice is beautiful too. And me. Me! She thinks I'm
good enough to sing with people like Marcia and
Debby."

"I'm not surprised," said my mother. "I always
thought you had a beautiful voice. I remember once
when you were about two and a half. We were in the
park and you began singing,

> Bobby Shaftoe's gone to sea
> Silver buckles on his knee
> He'll come back and marry me
> Pretty Bobby Shaftoe.

"You were so cute, standing there, singing at the top
of your lungs. And then this woman came over. She was
trying to get her baby to sleep, and she asked if you

110

could sing a little softer. I always thought it was such a pity because you were singing so beautifully, and you cried when she asked you not to sing so loud."

"Anyway," I continued, "the three of us are singing 'Three Little Maids from School Are We' from *The Mikado*. We take turns singing solo parts. I get to sing 'Life is a joke that's just begun,' in the first round and then later I get two more turns. It will be beautiful with our voices weaving in and out of each other's."

"It sounds lovely," said my mother.

"The three of us have to practice together," I said. "Mrs. Powers thinks we should probably wear kimonos. I told her I wanted to wear a blue one."

After dinner, Adam rang the bell and invited us upstairs to watch *Enemy Mine* on his VCR.

"It's supposed to be a great sci-fi picture with two enemies who crash land on a mysterious planet. One of them is a lizard-man. It sounds fantastic."

"Well, it's very nice of you to ask us, but I'm afraid I have to study for an English lit exam," my mother said. "But maybe Luke and Imo can watch."

"I'd like to," said my father, "but I promised Lin Lin I'd help her roll up her rug in the living room and move some of her furniture around."

"Why is she rolling up her rug?"

"Because her aerobics dance teacher lost her lease, and Lin Lin offered her apartment on Tuesday and Thursday evenings."

Adam said, "Your mother takes aerobic dancing?"

"Oh, yes," said my father. "She's really very good at it."

111

"But isn't it too strenuous for a woman her age?"

"Oh, Lin Lin never worries about her age."

"Lin Lin?" Adam said. "I was wondering why you called her Lin Lin."

My mother explained. "Her name is Linda, and when Luke was a baby he tried to say it, and it came out Lin Lin. His mother thought it was so cute that she decided that's what he should call her. And that's what we all call her."

"But didn't she ever want you to call her Mom?" Adam said.

"I call my mother Mom," I said. "And Adam, I can come see *Enemy Mine*. I'd like to see it. I'm ready. I just have to—uh—do something, but I'll be up in a few minutes."

I quickly changed into my blue fuzzy sweater with the boat neck, and began slapping makeup on my face. Yes, yes, yes, I did look something like Jennifer with my long face and dark hair. Maybe I didn't have her blue eyes, and maybe my nose was longer and my mouth larger, but the resemblance was striking, and it made me feel hopeful. "Beauty is in the eye of the beholder," my father always said. Which meant that if Adam had thought Jennifer's face pretty, maybe, maybe he would feel the same way about mine. And my nose wasn't running today either. I brushed mascara on my eyelashes, and then I leaned back and examined myself in the mirror. It was me all right, me, the soloist, me the girl with the shining, happy face in the mirror, me looking forward to watching *Enemy Mine* alone with Adam Derman upstairs in his apartment.

112

I think the movie was probably the worst one I'd ever seen in my whole life. Adam sat there entranced throughout. Once, when the lizard-man came slithering across the scene in a particularly revolting way, Adam turned toward me, grinned and squeezed my shoulder. Oh, it was glorious. The whole day was glorious. Maybe it was turning into the most glorious day in my life.

"Well?" Adam asked when it was over. "What did you think?"

"Oh, I thought it was—interesting."

"I thought so too. Maybe a little slow in the middle, but the rest of it was great."

"Yes," I said, "it was—interesting."

"You know, Imo, if you really enjoy sci-fi films, we can do this again. There's one called *Blade Runner.* All about Los Angeles in the twenty-first century. It's a real winner. I've seen it already but I wouldn't mind seeing it again if you're interested."

"Oh, yes," I told him, "I'd love to see it."

"Okay then." Adam smiled. What beautiful teeth he had. "Let's see—tomorrow I can't. I . . . I'm meeting a friend. And Wednesday . . . hmm . . . how about Thursday?"

"Thursday's fine."

"Or if another day next week is better . . ."

"No. Thursday's fine."

"So—it's a date. We'll turn you into a sci-fi addict." He laughed and I laughed. Then he said, "You're really looking very pretty today, Imo." He held his head over on one side, and looked at me through half-closed eyelids. Everything leaped around inside me. "That blue's a good color for you. I like blue."

"Really?"

"Yes. I always liked blue, and it suits you. But you're looking very happy today. Something special must have happened. Or maybe somebody special."

"No. Nobody special," I said quickly. "No. It's just that," I raced on, trying to avoid looking into his blue gray eyes, "it's just that I'm going to sing a solo in the final concert at school."

"Oh?"

"Well, you see, I never thought I had that good a voice, but Mrs. Powers, my chorus teacher, she thinks I've really improved. I'm going to be singing with a girl named Marcia Bingham. She's planning to go pro. I mean, I know I'm not that good, but . . ." I was chattering nervously, aware that Adam had moved closer to me.

"Now that's just great," Adam said, taking my hand. "What are you going to sing?"

Stop! I thought. Not to Adam but to time. Stop! Let this moment last forever and ever. Adam and I sitting in his living room, holding hands.

"Imo, what are you going to sing?"

"Oh, 'Three Little Maids from School Are We.'"

"What's that?"

"It's a song from *The Mikado.*"

"From what?"

"From *The Mikado.* By Gilbert and Sullivan."

"How does it go?"

He was holding on to my hand and I was feeling so

happy, not shy or awkward or silly, just happy. I wanted to sing, and I just opened my mouth and sang.

> Three Little Maids from school are we,
> Pert as a school-girl well can be,
> Filled to the brim with girlish glee
>   Three little maids from school!

"That's wonderful." Adam smiled and pressed my hand.

"Of course the three of us sing that part together."

"Lori sings," Adam said.

"My first real solo is 'Life is a joke that's just begun,' and later on I sing two more solos."

He was looking over my shoulder. "But she really doesn't have much of a voice. Kind of a monotone. Not like yours." Then he looked at me, smiled, bent over and kissed my forehead. Now I can die, I thought to myself.

"You're a good kid, Imo." Adam dropped my hand, and stood up. "And I'll see if I can get *Blade Runner* for Thursday. Ask your parents if they'd like to watch too."

"No," I told him. "They can't."

"Well, I could get it for another night. Maybe Friday. Oh wait, no . . . Friday's no good. But next week sometime?"

"They'll be busy next week," I said. "Thursday's fine."

Adam walked downstairs with me. "Benjamin's not coming over this weekend. Jennifer's taking him to L.A. Her grandparents are celebrating their 50th wedding anniversary, and she wants Benjamin to be there.

115

So you're home free for Saturday night. You can go out with your friends."

"I don't want to go out with my friends," I said.

"Why not?" Adam asked. We were standing in front of my door, and I was just about to slip my key in the lock. "I bet a girl like you has lots of friends. And I bet there's some special boy too, maybe in your chorus."

"No." I concentrated hard on the key. "No boy in my chorus. No boy period. I don't like boys my own age. They're so . . . so . . . young."

Adam laughed. I could feel his breath rippling across my ear, and I turned the key in the lock and hurried up the stairs.

Chapter 12 ᥅

I couldn't stop daydreaming about Thursday night.
About what I wanted to happen.

*"I'm afraid my VCR is broken, Imo. We won't be able
to watch* Blade Runner.*"*
*"That's all right, Adam. I'd just as soon sit here and
talk."*
*"Yes, I'd like that." He sat down next to me. The
gold chain on his bronze neck gleamed in the lamplight. "Or perhaps you'd sing for me again. I've been
thinking and thinking about your voice, so creamy
and smooth, like your skin, like your neck, like
your . . ."*

No, no!

"I'm afraid my VCR is broken, Imo. We won't be able to watch Blade Runner.*"*

"That's all right, Adam. I'd just as soon sit here and talk."

"Yes, I'd like that. I've been thinking about what you said Monday night. About boys. About boys being too young for you."

"Yes, boys are too young . . . too awkward . . . too gauche . . . too inexperienced."

"Because you're so mature . . . so extraordinary." *He took my hand and kissed it. The gold chain on his neck gleamed in the lamplight.*

I was dressed in my new blue sweater when Adam rang the bell after dinner on Thursday night.

"I'll get it," I shouted, hurrying downstairs. Adam stood there.

"I'm sorry, Imo," he said, "but I couldn't get *Blade Runner.* I went to two video places and both of them were out."

"Oh," I said, "well . . . that's okay. . . ."

"Maybe another time." Adam smiled and turned away.

"But . . . but . . ."

Adam paused, still smiling.

"Well . . . I was thinking . . . I never did see *The Empire Strikes Back.*" I didn't want to admit that I'd never actually sat through *Star Wars* either.

"Oh, you have to see *The Empire Strikes Back,*" Adam said solemnly.

"Well?"

"Well, if you're free tonight . . ."

118

"Yes," I said, "I'm free."

"Well, why don't you come upstairs and watch it then?"

"Okay. I'm coming. Right now."

"That's fine. The only thing is, when I couldn't get *Blade Runner*, I did call a friend of mine, and I am meeting her." Adam looked at his watch. "In about half an hour."

"Well, I can watch it another time then."

"No, no, I insist. There's no reason why you shouldn't watch it tonight. Come on up, and I'll get you set before I take off. I want you to make yourself at home in my house, Imo."

So I watched the *The Empire Strikes Back*. In between the phone calls from four different women, I watched it. And I began feeling sorry for myself. The new blue sweater was scratchy, and my neck itched.

"Linda called, and Renee, and Susan Phillips, and one called Margaret Hoffman," I told Adam when he returned. "She said she brought a white Honda Civic into your shop last Thursday, and you told her to let you know how it's running. She didn't tell me how it's running, but she left her number. She wants to tell you herself."

Adam shook his head, and sat down next to me. "I'm tired," he said. "I'm tired and I'm sick of it all."

I began feeling better. "Maybe you're coming down with a cold," I said.

Adam clenched his fist and punched the pillow next to him. "I don't want to live this way, running around every night of the week, wasting my time with women I don't care anything about. I'd rather do nothing. I'd rather stay home and do nothing." He looked at me. "I'd rather stay home and talk to you."

I licked my lips. "I thought *The Empire Strikes Back* was—interesting—very interesting."

He was looking at me, very hard. Staring. And I knew something big was about to happen.

"What's the matter with me, Imo?" he asked. "How did I get into all this?"

"Nothing's the matter with you," I cried. "You're . . . you're wonderful. You just haven't met anybody who understands you."

"That's what she said." Adam punched the pillow again.

"Who?"

"Jennifer. That's what she said when she decided to get a divorce. She said I didn't understand her. She said I never let her be herself. She said I wanted her to be somebody else. All I wanted was for her to clean the house and take care of Benjamin. All by herself. Was that unreasonable, Imo? I ask you, was I being unreasonable?"

"No," I cried. "Absolutely not. A woman should take care of her house and her family. She should cook good meals. It's only fair because her husband works hard and . . ." I thought of my own mother and father. What was I saying?

Adam drew closer. "That's just it, Imo. I never wanted her to be somebody else. She just didn't understand *me.*"

"Of course not," I said. "She's a very pleasant person. I can see that. But she's obviously not up to you. I mean, she seems—well—kind of—well—simple."

120

Adam nodded. "She is simple. But even with the ones who aren't—Lori, for instance. She's not simple, but she also says I don't understand women."

"That's absurd," I cried.

"What's to understand?" Adam said. "Women are people, like anybody else. I don't want all women to be the same. I never said they have to be the same."

"Of course not," I agreed heartily.

"All I say is that a woman isn't a man. Here's Lori, for instance, off on a vacation by herself. She's got lots of friends. Why did she have to go by herself? She's not afraid of anything. She doesn't use her head. She's much too independent."

"Oh, yes," I said. "I'm sure she is."

"She says I'm sexist. Just because I say she should be a little more careful. Just the way I told you to be careful that time you caught the thief. Is there anything wrong with looking out for a woman and trying to protect her?"

"Absolutely not!" I cried.

Adam smiled at me. "You are some kid, Imo. I really like you."

Pure bliss!

"And I like your family too. I don't really know your grandmother." Adam began laughing. "Imagine a woman her age going in for aerobic dancing! And that little orange VW bug downstairs? Is that really her car?"

"Yes it is," I said grimly, wishing Lin Lin was somebody else's grandmother.

"Your parents are great people—warm and friendly and very intelligent. Your mother now . . ."

121

"Yes?" I waited nervously for his question.

"What's she studying in school?"

"She's getting a master's degree in English literature. She has a master's in ancient history, but then she changed her mind after she got it. She decided she really was interested in English literature."

"Oh!" Adam said.

"When she first started school, she was interested in art. That's what she got her first B.A. in, but then she thought she really was interested in ancient history. She's always changing her mind and getting interested in something else."

"Oh!" Adam tried to look as if he understood, but I could see he didn't.

"She's very smart. She just likes studying."

"Well!" Adam laughed. "I guess there's no harm in that."

"No, I guess not." Then I started laughing too. But it wasn't a pleasant laugh. It was a mean laugh. As if I was laughing at my mother. As if I was ashamed of her.

"Now your father," Adam said. "He's quite a photographer."

"Oh, my father!" I said, still laughing that unpleasant laugh.

"Lori thinks he's very talented," Adam said. "And I do too, but . . ."

"But he doesn't make a living," I said, and suddenly I wasn't laughing anymore. I was crying. I was crying because I was really ashamed of my family—my mother, my father and Lin Lin. Maybe I'd always been ashamed of them, but never as I was right now, sitting in Adam Derman's living room and seeing them through his eyes.

"Imo," Adam said. "Imo, what is it?"

"My family is weird," I wailed. "We're not like other people. Nobody makes a living in my family. We live off the royalties of a book, *The Friendship Cookbook,* as a matter of fact. The one your mother owned. I never tell anybody, but my grandmother's aunt wrote the book."

"*The Friendship Cookbook*?" Adam repeated.

I was really howling. "I'm so ashamed of them," I wailed. "They can't cook. They're not interested in cooking. They never worry about money. Only I worry. That's why I have to be an accountant." My nose began running, and I took a furious swipe at it.

Adam moved closer to me, took one of my hands, the one that wasn't mopping my nose, and said, "I'm sorry, Imo. Don't mind me. I didn't mean to pry. I'm just in a lousy mood tonight. Everything I do is wrong. I can't do anything right today."

"My family's weird," I cried. "Maybe I'm weird too."

"No, no, no, Imo. You're not weird. You're a darling. You're smart and funny and you're great with kids. And you're pretty too."

"No, I'm not," I said, feeling the blue sweater itching. "Nobody thinks I'm pretty."

"Sure they do." Adam put an arm around me.

"Nobody thinks I'm pretty," I was crying again. "And my family's weird. Nobody's got a family as weird as mine."

"Don't say that." Adam patted my shoulder.

"I'm weirder than anybody I know," I wept. "And my allergies make me even weirder. My nose runs all the time—right in the middle of . . . well . . . who's ever going to love me the way my nose runs?"

Adam lifted my face and made me look right into his face. I stopped crying. Now it was happening. Now. My heart began pounding. My nose kept right on running, and I quickly dabbed at it. Now.

"Somebody loves you, Imo," Adam said softly.

Now.

"Running nose and all." Adam looked deep into my eyes.

I gulped, and inside me, something exploded. Something was thumping and bumping around. Is this what love, real love was all about?

"Somebody loves you best in the world."

No, it wasn't love, it was . . .

"Imo!" Adam moved closer.

Panic. It was panic.

"Benjamin loves you, Imo," Adam said. "I think he loves you better than me or Jennifer." Adam laughed. "Today when I spoke to him on the phone, he said, 'Imo,' not 'Daddy' or 'cookie.' He said, 'Imo. Gimme Imo.' But aside from Benjamin, you don't have to worry about attracting guys. I told you so before, Imo. You're a good, sweet, darling girl. I'm sure there are plenty of guys who like you and are just waiting for the chance."

I could have kissed him. No, I didn't want to kiss him. I didn't want him to kiss me either. No. He was too old for me, much too old. I realized it all of a sudden, sitting there close to him, having it nearly happen. I didn't want it to happen. I wasn't ready for it to happen.

Maybe it was okay in my daydreams, but it wasn't in real life.

"The thing is, they might feel a little overwhelmed by you. Because you're so smart. A lot of boys are nervous around a smart girl like you. I'm not saying don't be smart. What I'm saying is, give them a little encouragement. They're shy. You have to make them feel good about themselves. You have to . . ."

He went on and on, but I really wasn't listening to him. I was feeling happy, relieved and comfortable, and I didn't even mind that my nose went right on running.

"And another thing," Adam said, tightening his hold on my shoulder. "Don't ever feel ashamed of your own family."

"What?"

"Like you were saying before, Imo, that you thought your parents were weird. Don't ever say that about your own folks, even if . . ."

"Even if it's true," I giggled.

Adam frowned.

"Well," I told him, moving away, "I guess they are weird, but it's okay. I love them whatever they are. I just got a little mixed up there for a while, but I'm fine now."

Adam sighed. "I wish I were," he said.

He looked so downcast, I felt sorry for him. And grateful too. He was a nice man, a good man, and suddenly I wanted to do something for him. Because he was such a nice, good man and didn't love me at all.

"Listen, Adam," I said, "can I tell you something?"

"Why sure, Imo."

"I mean, you won't mind if I tell you what I think? You won't get angry because I'm only a kid?"

"You're very mature for your age, Imo. And I really respect your opinion."

"Well, Adam, if you want my honest opinion . . ."

"Sure, I do."

"I think you tend to go for the lowest common denominator."

"What?"

"I mean you keep being attracted to dopey women. Jennifer's nice, but there's not much going on upstairs. And Renee—well—Renee's not even nice. And those women who keep calling you up, I can hear from the way they speak, they're all birdbrains."

"Hey, Imo, just a minute, Imo!"

I moved closer to him and took his hand. "Adam, you're far from a stupid man."

"Thanks a lot."

I could see he was getting upset, so I said, "Maybe I should stop."

He shook his head. "No, no. Go ahead. Sooner or later, every woman I know tells me off. You might as well join the crowd."

"I'll tell you what my father thinks," I said.

"Your father?"

"My father thinks you like Lori."

"No, I don't." Adam shook his head. "We don't have anything in common."

"And my mother thinks she likes you."

"She does?"

"They both really liked her. They thought she was charming and intelligent and pretty too."

126

"Well, yes she is, but she's stubborn."

"So what?" I said.

"And I've known her since she was a kid."

"So what?"

Adam seemed to be thinking.

"She should be getting back from Hawaii soon," I said. "I know she's staying over for a few days before she goes back to Denver. Maybe you can get something going before she leaves. You might even end up having more things in common than you both realize. Just open your mind a little bit."

Adam said slowly, almost shyly, "Does your mother really think she likes me?"

"She's sure of it," I said, standing up. "I'd better go now, Adam. It was real nice of you to let me watch *The Empire Strikes Back.*"

"Oh." Adam shook his head slightly, and said, "That's right. I forgot you were watching *The Empire Strikes Back.* What did you think of it?"

"I hated it," I told him.

Chapter 13 ❧

The royalty check finally arrived, and it wasn't as bad as I had feared.

"You see," said my mother, "I told you not to worry. I told you something always turned up."

I shook my head. "Maybe you're right," I said. "It looks as if we'll be able to pay all our bills this time, and have a little bit over. Of course, we don't know what the next check will be like."

"It will probably be better," said my father. "Lin Lin forgot to tell us but she's been asked to serve on the board of directors of a new cooking school that's opening in Minneapolis."

"Cooking school? Lin Lin?"

"Yes. They called her the day of the robbery, but in all the excitement she forgot to mention it. The school will be called The Friendship Cooking School, and *The*

Friendship Cookbook will be the text for all the students. They're hoping to open other schools all over the country."

"I can't believe this," I said. "Lin Lin doesn't know how to cook. Why should they want her on the board?"

"She's going to be the speaker at a banquet when the school opens," my father said proudly. "They want her to reminisce about her aunt. And they're going to pay her an honorarium too."

"It's crazy," I told Melissa later that day, over the phone. "My grandmother doesn't even know how to fry an egg properly."

"Well anyway," Melissa said, "now you can stop worrying, can't you?"

"I guess so, for the time being. But now they're spending the money before it even arrives. My father wants a new camera, my mother says she's going to go on for a Ph.D., and Lin Lin . . ." I groaned. "Lin Lin says she wants to buy a red Corvette."

"She really is sweet," Melissa said, "even if she can't fry an egg."

"Yes," I admitted. "I think so too."

"Anyway, Imo, I've been meaning to talk to you about something else."

I laughed. "I know. I know, Melissa. You want to set me up with Leo."

"No," Melissa said. "No, I don't."

"It's okay, Melissa. I'm not going to jump all over you. I've been thinking, and maybe it's not such a bad idea. Maybe the four of us can double-date this weekend. I'm free this weekend."

"What happened to the man upstairs?" Melissa

asked. "I thought you weren't interested in boys."

"I changed my mind. I decided he was too old for me. I even told him he should look for a woman his own age."

"You mean *you* broke it off?"

"We're still friends," I said. "But anyway, Melissa, now that Leo's voice changed, I really see that he has possibilities. I mean he's a big, awkward lug, but I guess he is sweet, and he does have a marvelous sense of humor."

"Oh yes," Melissa said, "he does."

"So anyway, I'm ready."

There was silence at the other end of the line.

"And I'm free this Saturday."

More silence.

"But if this Saturday's no good, I'm also free next Saturday. I might have to sit for Adam on Sunday, but if that's better, maybe I can change."

"No, no," Melissa said, "it's not that."

"Well, what is it?"

Melissa took a long, deep breath. "You see, Imo, it's like this— In the beginning, I used to talk to Leo about you. Sometimes, we'd talk in school and sometimes over the phone. I think he really liked you, but you weren't interested. Anyway, I used to encourage him to keep trying. And then after a while, we got to talking about other things. At first we talked maybe a couple of nights a week, and then three or four times, and finally every night. All the time, his mother would be yelling in the background. Sometimes we'd just spend the time laughing. He's so funny. I feel good just talking to him. But then, Jeff got sore. . . ."

"Jeff?"

"Yes, he got jealous."

"Jeff? Jealous of Leo? That's incredible."

"I don't know," Melissa said stiffly, "why it should be so incredible."

"Well, Jeff is gorgeous and Leo . . . well, Leo is . . ."

"Leo . . ." Melissa said softly, "that's just what I'm trying to tell you, Imo. Leo's the greatest guy I ever met. He doesn't have a phony bone in his whole body. He's all up front. He's smart and sensitive . . . and you said you weren't interested in him. And now even his mother likes me." Melissa giggled. "She says his voice changed because he kept talking to me every night on the phone. She doesn't yell anymore."

"Melissa," I said, "don't tell me you and Leo . . ."

"Yes," she said, "isn't it wonderful?"

I sat in Dr. Rovensky's office, pretending to read the latest issue of *Today's Health*, but watching Mark Feller out of the corner of my eye.

Mrs. Foster was telling Mr. Helling about her friend's dog who developed beefy, red rashes between his toes, and had to be treated with antihistamines before he improved.

Mark was working away at what might have been his math homework. His backpack was thrown in the chair next to his, but he took it away and pushed it under his seat as Mrs. Jackson and Bobby came into the waiting room. Bobby ran over to me, pulled my head down, and whispered in my ear that he and his classmates were working on Mother's Day cards, and that I shouldn't tell his mother.

"I was hoping to see you today, Imo," said Mrs. Jackson. "Can you come a little earlier tomorrow night and give Bobby his dinner?"

"Sure," I said.

"Bobby says Imo is the best cook in the world," Mrs. Jackson announced to the office. "He never eats with me the way he does with her."

I knew that Mrs. Jackson was a gourmet cook and was pained that Bobby preferred my cooking to hers.

"And then I wondered if you had any evenings free this weekend. I know you usually sit for the man up-stairs on one night and are busy with your friends on the other. But I wondered if you could make an exception this weekend."

"Well . . ." I began.

Mrs. Jackson headed me off. "If you want to have a friend over, Imo, that would be all right. Even a boy-friend."

Now why did she have to say that? I certainly did not want Mark Feller to think I had a boyfriend.

"I don't have a boyfriend," I said.

And why did I have to sound so fierce about it? Maybe Mark would assume I was the kind of girl who wasn't interested in having a boyfriend. I didn't want him to think that either.

"Not now," I said.

"What?" Mrs. Jackson asked.

"I don't have a boyfriend *now*," I mumbled, feeling my cheeks grow warm. It was getting more and more out of hand, I thought. Just tell her you can sit for her and then shut up, which I did.

"Mark Feller," Adrian called out.

132

He stood up and followed her into the office. Mrs. Jackson asked if she could go next because she was parked in a red zone. I sighed. Mr. Helling, Mrs. Foster and a couple of other people were ahead of me. It didn't seem as if the boy and I would ever be alone together in the office, would ever be able to strike up a conversation. Only in daydreams, I thought, did everything work out as it should.

"You're looking very well today, dear," said Mrs. Foster. "That shade of blue is particularly flattering."

"Thank you, Mrs. Foster," I said. "I never used to wear blue, but now I think it's one of my favorite colors."

Other people had commented on how well I looked in blue. Only this morning, Mrs. Powers had agreed that I could wear a blue kimono at the final concert. "It's such a good color for you," she said.

Each of us is wearing a soft, pastel-colored kimono on the stage—pale yellow, pale pink, and myself in pale blue. Our voices rise and fall, and, out there in the audience, a hush falls as one voice rises pure and high above all the others, one voice singing "Life is a joke that's just begun." There is a motionless figure seated in the first row, his upturned face filled with rapture, his eyes glued to mine. Yes it is he, the boy in the office. It is Mark Feller.

I settled myself back comfortably inside my daydream, and let the office conversations continue without me.

"Imogen Rogers, last but not least," Adrian called out

finally. And I rose, shaking off the magic in an empty waiting room. As I followed her into the office, I pushed up the sleeve of my sweater.

"You're looking very pretty today, Imogen," Adrian said, giving me my shot. "I really like that color on you."

"Thank you, Adrian," I said. "I guess I'll be wearing it a lot from now on."

I put on my jacket and stepped outside. It was raining. Even though we were in the middle of May when it's not supposed to rain, it was raining. Hard. I stood there in the doorway, blinking at the raindrops bouncing up off the street, and wondering if I should stay where I was until it stopped, or just make up my mind that I would get drenched, and head for the bus stop.

"Excuse me," somebody said.

"Oh!" It was Mark Feller who came running into the doorway from the street. His hair was dripping with raindrops, and he said breathlessly, "I left my backpack in the office."

"Oh!" I said again, looking up into his face. He was even taller than Leo, and his eyes were a deep shade of brown.

"Isn't this rain crazy?" he said, not making any move to open the door into the waiting room.

"Oh yes," I agreed heartily. "It never rains in May."

"Well, I remember one time it did. Maybe a couple of years ago."

"Is that so?"

"Yes," he said, looking over my head. "I remember. It was in the middle of May. Just like now."

He really was a very pleasant-looking boy, even if he didn't seem particularly comfortable at the moment.

134

Wasn't it lucky that he had forgotten his backpack.

"Maybe I do remember it raining a couple of years ago," I said encouragingly. "Yes, now that I think of it, I do remember."

Mark Feller stood there, looking over my head. Then he said, "You know, I've been meaning to tell you something."

"Really?" I said. "What is it?"

He began smiling, and his eyes dropped down to the top of my head. "She really does have one brown eye and one blue eye," he said.

"Who does?"

"Dr. Rovensky. Remember you told little Bobby Jackson she did a few months ago. And I've been meaning to tell you that it's true."

Mark Feller and I were standing there together in the doorway of Dr. Rovensky's office. He had just spoken to me, actually spoken to me, and his words were fraught with enchanting possibilities. It was like being in a daydream. No. It was better than being in a daydream.

"I don't think the rain is going to stop for a while," I told him. "Why don't we go back inside the office and wait until it does."